ATLANTIS IS PANDORA'S BOX

ATLANTIS IS PANDORA'S BOX

Fantasies about Sherlock Holmes nowadays

Book 7

By Sophia Kiev

This book is a work of fiction. The references to the real places, the historical events, are used fictitiously. All names, characters, places and events are fictional. Any resemblances to actual events, places, or persons are coincidental. The book used stories from the Bible and the Tales of the Miracles of the Kazan Icon of the Mother of God.

ISBN—9798588413374

https://sophiakiev.com

sophiakievukraine@gmail.com

Table of Contents

INTRODUCTION --- 7

CHAPTER I: DID A SMUGGLER FOUND ATLANTIS? --------------- 9

CHAPTER II: THE SMUGGLER'S DAUGHTER---------------------- 16

CHAPTER III: TRAGIC FATE OF THE SCUBA DIVERS------------ 21

CHAPTER IV: JOURNEY AND INVESTIGATION UNDER
DISGUISE --- 27

CHAPTER V: HOW TO FIND THE DOOR TO THE BUNKER? ---- 37

CHAPTER VI: INGLORIOUS DEATH OF THE SMUGGLER------- 43

CHAPTER VII: REVENGE AS AN EASY METHOD OF HUMAN
MANIPULATION -- 49

CHAPTER VIII: STUNNING RESULT OF THE EXPERTISE ------- 60

CHAPTER IX: UNEXPECTED MEETING WITH THE DEATH ---- 65

CHAPTER X: BIG FISH SWALLOWED THE SMALL ONE -------- 76

CHAPTER XI: LOOKING FOR DISAPPEARED EVIDENCE ------- 83

CHAPTER XII: CRIMINAL WITH NICKNAME DRUNK QUIET -- 89

CHAPTER XIII: WHO IS BRAZILIAN WANDERER? ---------------- 95

CHAPTER XIV: NO SIGNS OF TROUBLE----------------------------104

CHAPTER XV: SHE HAD TO DIE -------------------------------------113

CHAPTER XVI: THE AUTHENTIC STORY OF TREASURE
HUNTERS ---120

CHAPTER XVII: DID GOD CURSE ATLANTES? -------------------147

ABOUT THE AUTHOR ---159

THE OTHER BOOKS WRITTEN BY SOPHIA KIEV----------------161

Introduction

This is the seventh book from the series of fiction about the adventures of Sherlock Holmes nowadays.

Someone put up the statue Nereid riding on a dolphin at a black auction. This event alerted Holmes. He suspected that one smuggler entered the game. Holmes has been observing his action for about six years now. According to Holmes's research, this person found lost civilization five years ago. But proximately in one year, something went wrong, and this man finished selling artifacts. He turned into the addicted gambler and lost his entire fortune in a short time. Two days ago, someone robbed his partner when he was driving home from the bank. For Holmes's surprise, the partner's daughter hired him to investigate her father's case.

This investigation led to the chain of the others investigating which related to discovering the lost Empire, and caused the battle with the criminal mind, who obsessed with greediness for enrichment. Except for the major task, he has the second desire — to kill Holmes. For this aim he used his manipulative skills and convinced narrow-minded woman to help set a trap for the detective.

The unexpected accidents accompanied the investigation all but every day. Our investigators had not enough time to have a rest. Events unfolded in such a way that chasing criminals, Holmes found them already dead. The mysterious deaths of the people started about five years ago and continue till now. The first person, the Cypriot man, died in the end of the first month from the beginning of the searching for the lost world of Atlantis. One person died about three years ago. Two people — over the month ago. Almost everyone who had a deal with Atlantis, died.

There is the ancient legend which Cypriots pass on from generation to generation.

"According to this legend, God forbade to look for this island. He punished the people from the island for their grave sins by immersing their civilization in the depths of the sea. They violated the traditions, transmitted by their ancestors, and lost the moral qualities which they originally endowed with. Degradation occurred. It led to the decline of the entire Atlantis empire. If anyone dares to look for Atlantis, the God's punishment will befall him. Just as the sea waves swallowed Atlantis, so a naughty person will suffer sudden death."

Are the deaths of the people connected with an ancient legend, or the criminal mind is covering his tracks and destroying the evidence pointed at him?

"Do not follow your inclination and strength
in pursuing the desires of your heart.
Do not say, "Who can have power over me?"
for the Lord will surely punish you."
Book of the Wisdom of Jesus, the Son of Sirach 5, 2-3

Chapter I: Did a smuggler found Atlantis?

- Watson. What do you think about this part of sculpture?
- It's head of a woman, which was made from gold.
- You are very observant. But you are wrong. This is not gold. Something tells me this is orichalcum.
- I've never heard about it. What is this metal and where is it mined?
- It doesn't exist on the Earth any more. Take a closer look at this coin and say: which country issued such coins? I give you a hint: it's ancient.
- I don't particularly understand numezmatism and the artifacts of antiquity. There are a lot of documentaries about this, and I like it. But no whiter than that. If you know something, I'll gladly listen to your story, or theory about these things.
- Orichalcum is a mysterious metal, or maybe it's rather an alloy. The news of him came to us in the works of the most ancient Greek authors. Josephus reports that the sacred vessels in the temple of Solomon were made of this metal. The difference lies because Plato writes in his work "Critias" that the orichalcum is a native mineral extracted from the

9

bowels of the earth. In its value, the orichalcum was second only to gold. Other sages, who lived after Plato, wrote that it was an alloy of copper and calcium. As for sculpture and coins, I suggest starting with a coin. You can then understand why I came to such incredible conclusions. The coin is also made of orichalcum. On one side of it is a man with a trident in his hand. This is how ancient Greek mythology depicted the Poseidon. Back to the sculpture. If you look closely, this is not a complete work, but a small part of something. I guess this is Nereid, a mermaid woman. According to Plato's work "Critias", there were one hundred sculptures of Nereids riding on dolphins in the temple of Poseidon. This temple was on the island of Atlantis. If we consider two objects together, sculpture and coin, then the conclusion suggests itself: they have one place of origin. Namely from Atlantis.

■ Where did you find these photos?

■ This is not just a photo; my dear friend. These are exhibits. Someone put up them at a black auction last night. Their value has a fabulous amount. Of all this history, only one conclusion suggests itself: Tyrin George found Atlantis.

■ If Atlantis was found, this news would spread fast all around the world. Don't you think?

■ It's not a fact. This would do for a man who is chasing a sensation or wanting to glorify his name. But the smuggler doesn't need it. He obsessed of money.

■ Anyway, who is Tyrin?

■ O. This is the ambassador, whom I have been observing for about six years now. Nine years and a half ago, ancient objects appeared on sale on the black market, such as amphorae, Italian copper jugs and coffee pots, smoking pipes. But most of all, Chinese porcelain from the Ming Dynasty was in demand. It lasted a little more than three years. Interpol could not find the owner of these goods. Information popped up in fits and starts after the auction. It was impossible to find the new owners of ancient artifacts. When I analyzed this information, I made the conclusion: the corruption was blossoming, and no one looked for anything. Undoubtedly, the owner of the artifacts dependent on the authorities. And these high-ranking officials, allegedly fighting smuggling, showed photos in the press for imitation of their work. But this imitation was also carried out to intimidate or blackmail the owner of the goods. They simply pointed him at his place. If he disobeys, they will have dealt with him at any moment. Why did I draw such a conclusion? It's elementary.

In about three years later, Ukrainian Ambassador to Spain Tyrin George made an announcement about the sensational discovery of several sunken ships with treasures at the bottom of the Mediterranean Sea. According to him, he is an amateur diver. That year, he spent his holidays in the Balearic Islands, namely on the island of Cabrera. As you know, these islands are in Spanish jurisdiction. And for Mr. Tyrin, it was not a problem to go with his family to rest there. He received a prize in the form of a decent amount from the Spanish government for finding ships with jewelry.

Since then, I have been watching him. Later I found out about his companion. Anton Tyutkin is the owner of a restaurant business in the city of Nikolayev in southern Ukraine. He also owns art and sculpture galleries in Odessa on Derebasovskaya Street. You should note, this is a suitable street for this kind of activity. It is in the city center. There are many attractive restaurants, cafes and shops on this street.

So here. What am I leading to? Four years and a half ago, someone put up an amazing exhibit at a sculpture auction in London - a sea nymph riding a dolphin. An unknown nugget sculptor from Odessa made this artwork. According to his interview, he was so carried away by reading Plato's dialogue "Critias" that he decided to realize some sculptures described. His first work was the head of a flying horse. This sculpture attracted the attention of Anton Tyutkin. He bought the exhibit and put it on display in his gallery. Just this event coincided with the birthday of Plato. I think you can guess how many people, who are fond of the works of Plato, came to admire the sculpture. Success turned a head to a previously unknown sculptor. And he decided to create something more impressive. His choice fell on Nereid riding a dolphin. To do this, he even donated money and covered the sculpture with a thin layer of gold. The triumph was indescribable. His name was full in all European newspapers and on the Internet. Yesterday he was an unknown person, and at the top of fame today. He sold the sculpture for a fabulous amount to the American museum for one billion dollars.

The amount attracted my attention. Why so expensive? I searched for information on the Internet. What I found surprised me. About a half a year before the auction in London, someone showed on the Internet a photo of a coin with imprinting of Poseidon. There were many responses. Some people said it was a cool reproduction; the other — it's a graphic. To tell the truth, the photo was taken in such a way, you could make assumption towards the last conclusion. But I have a program which can distinguish graphics from the original. The result of the program was rouse: it was the original. The chain has closed. This could not be a coincidence. I searched by IP address of the owner of the photo. It turned out to be a young man from the Republic of Cyprus. He lived in Kouklia. This village is about 16 kilometers south of the city of Paphos. I went to Cyprus with a desire to meet him. My trip was unsuccessful, since he was not alive. According to his parents, he drowned in the sea. He died two months after posting the malicious photograph. I went to Odessa and visited the gallery of sculptures of Mr. Tyutkin. And failure awaited me there too. He sold the sculpture immediately after the celebration of Plato. The gallery manager explained that someone offered to the director the seductive amount of money for the sculpture that he could not resist. It is clear, no one knows anything about the buyer. This information was strictly confidential.

When I flew home from Cyprus, an interesting thought came to my head: where is Tyrin George now working? In all actions, it seems, he lives in the Cyprus region. My guesses proved. Five years ago, he was transferred as ambassador to Cyprus. This happened soon after the photo with a coin appeared on the Internet. From this moment, I was sure — Atlantis was found about five years ago. If I were wrong, then there would be no point in hiding the buyers of sculptures and coins. Because no one knows the buyers where being, it's impossible to do the test from which metal the sculptor made the statues and the coins. The question arises: why did they display the statue now with almost five years' break?

■ According to your assumptions, Atlantis is in the Mediterranean Sea. But many scientists consider her location in the Atlantic Ocean. I know there are many theories. There are a lot of documentary movies on the Internet. Some put Atlantis even in the Black Sea. I consider this theory the most incredible. Even Brazil, by its location, is more suitable for this.

■ I know. When I was looking for the answer on my question about Atlantis, I found one article. I did not agree with an author, but the time proved his righteous. The author placed Atlantis into the Mediterranean Sea. His explanations were simple. First, he used Plato's work "Critias" as a lighthouse. According to Plato, Atlantis had a war with Athens. Since there were no ships that could sail far, and the navigation didn't exist then, the war could take place only in the Mediterranean Sea. Second, because in ancient times, the main navigable mouth of the Nile was also called the Pillars of Hercules, an author considered that Plato mentioned exactly these pillars in his work. He referred to Timotheus's words that the residues after sinking Atlantis prevented the way "from them into the open see". Since he told about Egypt, it witnessed the location of Atlantis. If you look at the map, you'll see the Mediterranean Sea before the Egypt. Third, according to Plato's words, silt, which remained as residues from the disaster, was spread into the sea, and during some time disappeared. That's why, an author placed Atlantis in front of outfall of Nile; between islands Crete, Cyprus and the north shore of Africa. Moreover, according to observation the bottom of the sea from the space, there is a hollow in this place.

■ It looks like a truth. Did you ask the man's parents from Cyprus about his death?

■ Sure. They refused to speak with me. I only heard one sentence: he was punished from God for his disobedience. We can only guess what had happened. According to my assumption, this man somehow found out about Atlantis's existence. He was a scuba diver, but for this aim he needed a bathyscaphe. This is higher level than he could reach. The sea is deep in this area, it's about 3000-4000 meters. He decided to find a sponsor. The first thing, what he could do, was to place the photo of coin on the Internet. Many people considered this information as a joke and didn't pay close attention. But Tyrin was different. He felt good profit and contacted with the man. They agreed to work together, but something went wrong, and Tyrin got rid of this poor man. Or this man drowned, as his parents said. Being an ambassador of Cyprus, Tyrin could easily put his goods on the ship and transfer to Ukrainian freight port in Odessa or Illichivsk. His friend and accomplice has sculptures gallery in Odessa. It's the simplest way for smuggling.

■ Can we take them to the justice?

■ Who knows? For this aim, we need to have some information, but not my guessing.

■ Where is Tyrin now?

■ Tyrin retired four years ago. I find strange his early retirement. It would seem he only discovered Atlantis, and he had a lot of work. And suddenly — a pensioner. Somehow all this does not fit into one heap. Soon he turned into an avid gambler and has squandered his entire fortune into gambling. He is lucky to have a large pension, but for a gambler, it is not enough to satisfy all his whims.

- What about Tyutkin?
- Three years ago, thieves attacked his house. They were armed. His daughter escaped and call the police. But while the police arrived, Tyutkin's wife was killed. After this incident, Tyutkin guarded himself with many guards. People judged him he had a persecution mania. He could no longer carry out his business on his own. Because of this, his daughter was included on the board of companies and was appointed to the position of deputy director. Since this time, she went on business trips and concluded contracts. Her father led the entire process through video communications. For the past three years, he has not left his city. By the way, the day before yesterday, there was news about him. Someone again attacked Tyutkin. He was driving home from the bank. The daughter was on a business trip in London. According to correspondents, a nervous breakdown occurred with him, because he constantly asked someone for forgiveness and seemed to see some hallucinations. Unfortunately, it was impossible to make out his speech clearly. They took this interview upon Tyutkin's arrival at the hospital. But when his lawyer arrived, the interview ceased. It is only known that he is in the neurological department of the central hospital of Nikolayev. Doctors hide his diagnosis by referring to the medical confidentiality of patient information.

Chapter II: The smuggler's daughter

The doorbell interrupted our conversation. In a few minutes', beautiful lady crossed the threshold of our living room. Missis Hudson introduced her as Lydia Tyutkin. WOW! It looked like the sequel of Holmes's story. We greeted each other. Holmes invited her to sit down.

- What can I do for you, miss Lydia? — Holmes asked.
- I want to hire you for the investigation of my father's accident. Unknown people robbed him on his way home from the bank. This happened at about 4pm on the road between the Greenhouse and Vegetable Plant and the office of SVT- "Pine". There are no cameras on the road. Thieves blocked the road with the car immediately after turning near the office of SVT- "Pine". The father's driver didn't expect to meet the obstacle and braked sharply. The car stopped almost at the car of criminals. They rushed to the father's car. According to the driver, there were five of them. Two pulled the driver out of the car and beat him. Three rushed to pull out my father from the car and took the jewelry. Father held the suitcase in his arms. It looked like the robbers knew about the father's plans in advance and planned the robbery. The men wore the masks. It was impossible to make out the faces. The driver is in the hospital. He has many beatings and a concussion.
- It is clear, the driver could not see the car numbers. But he could remember the color and model of the car.

■ He said it was a silver old sedan. In addition, in the territory of our house there is a swimming pool. More precisely, he was until the day before yesterday. When I returned from a business trip, I immediately went to the hospital to my father. I got home late in the evening. The pool is located a little farther behind the house. Arriving home exhausted, I ate and went to bed. Yesterday morning, I went for a swim. But, as it turned out, someone pumped out water from the pool and deepened it another twenty meters. I called the police, but they found nothing. There are prints of tractor tires and a large truck. We have a courtyard with outbuildings further behind the pool. There is also a gate to another entrance.

■ What did your father take from the bank?

■ My father was a lover of antiques. He kept the most precious things in a bank cell. The day before yesterday morning, he took these antiques from the bank and drove home.

■ Why was he alone? Where were his guards?

■ My father didn't want to attract the attention by the presence of guards. He left them at home.

■ Do you know what things were in the bank?

■ These were old gemstone necklaces, gold rings, gemstones, ancient coins and gold bars with engravings and inscriptions. A lot of different. You can't list everything.

■ Do you mean the same coins, from which someone made the necklace that is now on your neck?

Holmes and Lydia continued their conversation. I observed her necklace. It looked familiar to me. When I looked closer, I got it. Holmes described me earlier one of them. He insisted it was from Atlantis. Unfortunately, the lady's beauty impressed me, and I didn't pay attention at the right things. I have to learn a lot from Holmes. Let's return to the conversation.

- Yes. How do you know these are an ancient?
- Every detective has to know such stuff. Why did he decide to take them home? Did someone threaten him?
- Hard to tell. After the attack on our house three years ago, my father developed a persecution mania. On this basis, he sometimes saw hallucinations. He constantly asked for forgiveness from them. From this event, he put all precious things to the bank.
- Hallucinations accompanied by a conversation with men or women?
- He was talking to men. According to father, he did wrong to them and was very guilty. He also swore he would free them. But from where he was going to free them, he didn't say. Father called four names and two surnames: Fedot, Avdeev, Peter, Taras, Murzya and Vadim.
- That's interesting. Did you tell this information to the detective?
- He didn't ask. The police always look at the hallucination as an illness and don't pay close attention on it. After conversation with the doctor, he didn't listen to me either. The doctor diagnosed my father with paranoid schizophrenia.
- O. I see. What was inside the pool?
- I don't know. Do you think something was there?
- I am sure about it. At least, they tried to find something. If they have not found what they were looking for, they'll do the other attempt. Did they intrude inside the house?
- I didn't observe the mess. All seemed as always.
- You have to look more carefully. May you find something disappeared from the house. Or if thieves didn't find under the pool what they were looking for, they'll return looking for this thing inside the house. It's obviously.
- After returning home, I'll do what you told me.
- When did your father decide to take home precious stuff?
- It's about a month.

- What prompted him to make such a decision? Did some stranger came to him, or he was blackmailed?
- He has never explained his decisions. It was just an announcement. My father is a confident person. He need not someone's approval to his action. Will you come to Nikolayev?
- Sure. Tomorrow morning we'll be there. Leave your address and telephone number. May we'll go by the same train.
- It's impossible. What's time is it? — She looked at her watch. — O. It's about 12pm. My flight in two hours and a half. The taxi is waiting for me. I need to be at home today. It's not good to leave my father and business for a long time without ruling.

With these words we said goodbye to each other and she left.

- Such a beautiful and intelligent woman. — I said with admiration.
- I noticed nothing attractive, except the necklace with the coins from the Atlantis.
- How can you judge so strictly about a woman at first sight?
- Have you seen the series of the Odessa Film Studio "Prisoner of If Castle"?
- Is it based on the novel by Alexander Dumas, "Count of Monte Cristo"?
- Yes. So, she looks like the daughter of the banker Baron Danglar.
- You made an impressive comparison. Poor woman.
- Can you explain to me: why she hired me to investigate her father's case?
- She wants to find the thieves and jewelries. It's obvious. — Holmes's question surprised me.
- Really? I would not be so sure about it. She knows well, her father transferred these ancient artifacts to Ukraine illegally. Do you think Lydia doesn't realize if we find the jewelries, we'll take the artifacts from them? As a result, her father will be sentenced and will send to

the prison. She will be punished too as an accomplice. Doesn't that strike you as suspicious? Or do you think she knows nothing about her father's deals? If it's so. The next question: how could he appointed her as the deputy of the director if she knows nothing? A? According to her words, he is ruling entire process from his house using the internet.

- I didn't think this way.
- Well. I need to work.

Holmes went to his lab. I stayed in the living room, thinking about his words. He can be right. She is a very attractive woman and a rich. How can I expect she will look at my side? And Holmes's suspicious about this investigation. Surely he is the best in this field. But if he is right, why she came here and hired us? That's strange. We'll see.

Chapter III: Tragic fate of the scuba divers

I t was about 4pm, when Holmes came to the living room. As always, he came up with the news.

■ An interesting business is brewing, Watson. We'll investigate the robbery of the criminal. They expect help from us. But as a result, the victim himself will end up in the dock. Although, because of the illness, he will certainly be able to shorten his term.

■ Can you prove Tyutkin's participation in the sale of antiques?

■ Let's not get ahead of ourselves. It all depends on the facts that we can collect. And the people we can find alive.

■ Has anyone already died?

■ Yes, my friend. It is regrettable to talk about this, but witnesses in this case may not live to see the trial. Two are already dead, not counting the man from Cyprus. I started checking from social networks. Many people boast about their accomplishments, having a wonderful vacation on exotic islands and much more, which is not worth boasting about. The thieves often find goals for their dirty tricks in social networks. Their victims are boastful persons who put on display acquired last-minute packages to resorts. Also, these narrow-minded people announce the period till which they cannot appear on social networks. In this connection, many victims began to warn about these mistakes and to request not to put personal information on public display. It's better to do this upon arrival. But this is not the best option. There is a proverb: "What you brag about, you will stay without it. Happiness loves silence". And this proverb works clearly without a miss.

So. Lydia announced to us people's names and surnames. I looked for them using the filter "scuba diver" or "scuba diving enthusiast". This filter was chosen as the basis, because our two wealthy adventurers could be interested only in people with such skills. I doubt they dived into the water to get the jewelries by themselves. And I found four people who matched my selection. For some reason they had not used their pages in the social medias four years. Their names are Taras Avdeev, Fedot Govorkov, Peter Shchusev and Vadim Korotkov. One of them, Taras Avdeev, came to the page a month ago. He was looking for Tyrin and Tyutkin. But Tyrin doesn't use social networks. Whereas Tyutkin uses all kinds of social networks to promote his business. Surely, he was looking for their addresses. I could not find one person with the surname Murzya.

Then, I checked from where Tyutkin was going to free people when he had hallucinations. In this case, there are two options: the first — they were accused of smuggling antiques instead of our rich criminals and sent to prison with promising: they will help to reduce their sentences; the second option — poor divers were put in a psychiatric hospital. Four years ago, something happened. Tyrin couldn't just retire from such a hot spot. And it's not just for nothing these people didn't use their pages on social networks four years. I was right.

It is easy to check whether they are in prison. During this search, I found that two people from our list, Avdeev Taras and Vadim Korotkov, have been on the wanted list for more than a month. They were in a psychiatric hospital in the city of Mariupol. Two days before the incident, the doctor changed the medicine for them. For some reason, these four people felt bad. Two of them, Peter Shchusev and

Fedot Govorkov, died. The ambulance took Taras and Vadim to the intensive care unit of the central city hospital. They stayed alive. But the doctors didn't establish strict observation for them in the intensive care unit. Men seized the opportunity and fled at night. This happened on the night of July 11-12, i.e. on the night of Sunday to Monday. According to the information from the police, they were placed in a mental hospital four years ago with a diagnosis of paranoid schizophrenia. When I hear this diagnosis, it alarms me. If we analyze the course of events, then everyone, who is objectionable, such as these men or Valentina Saulyak from Lvov, is given this diagnosis.

Looking through the police's wanted list, I looked through the list of missing people. Surprisingly, I found the fifth person — Murzya Ivan. But I can be wrong. It's only my speculation. There is no his page on the Facebook. We need to find out the name of the fifth person. By the way, Watson, get ready. This evening train at 22:14 we are going on a business trip. — The Holmes's smartphone made a sound that notified of the receipt of the letter. — Great. Gregson didn't let me down. You remember, his confidant works in the road patrol service. In order not to lose time, I requested information from the city cameras of Nikolayev and the village where Tyutkin lives. According to Lydia, someone used a tractor and a large truck to transport cargo, which was hidden under the pool. Such a large technique could not evaporate in the air. The cameras had to record their movement. I'll need your help. We'll looking for the cars whose DVR recorders recorded the movement of thieves. It would not surprise me if on the truck we see the second statue of Nereid sitting on a dolphin. All this suggests: Tyrin again entered the game. But for some reason, this time they are selling the statue not in its entirety, but in a split form. Or it was just a lure. And later they will show the entire picture on the day of the exhibit. Who knows? We'll see.

In addition, I don't like Lydia's correspondence with the unknown. After leaving our house, she reported to someone about hiring me for investigation. And she advised this person to prepare for a meeting. It looks like a trap.

- Knowing this is a trap, are you still going to go there, anyway?
- It has become even more interesting than before. The question is, her respondent's phone number served by an American telecom operator.
- Are you hinting me this is the professor Moriarty's trap?
- Indeed. If I am right, it explains why Lydia hired me to investigate this case. She is sure the criminals will kill me. But we must outwit them. Obviously, they plan to arrange an explosion in the train. I bought tickets through online. They undoubtedly have a good hacker and they know when we are going, the number of our carriage and compartment, by which we'll go. I spoke with Mycroft. He'll send his people. They will arrest the criminal. We'll leave the train on the first stop. Steve will wait for us nearby the railway station. Further, we'll travel by his car. The criminals saw Timur's car in the Enerhodar. We cannot risk. Moreover, Steve will be more helpful in this investigation than Timur. He is IT person, and he knows well CCTV cameras.

 After our arrival, we'll not go straight away to Tyutkin. Let Lydia think her plan was successful. On the news will be announced about the incident on the train Rivne-Nikolayev. During the time we won, we must dig up quickly into this case as much as we can. I sent Lydia's phone book to my friend, because I have no time to fulfill so many tasks at once. He will look with whom she talks. And perhaps he will find something interesting in her correspondence.

- When we'll arrive to Nikolayev, we must work. For this aim, want we or not, but we'll meet Lydia and her father. She'll warn her accomplice about our place of stay. We'll provoke hunt again. Will we be all right?
- Don't worry. We with Mycroft planned every step which we can predict. He has his people in Odessa and he'll send them to Nikolayev.

When we'll arrive to the city, they'll arrange accommodation for us. We'll work and live there. Also, they'll back up us. Surely we can meet something unpredictable. No one is safe from this. Now let's work.

Long hours of viewing the recordings from the city cameras of Nikolayev and Balovnoye stretched. Our heroine with her father lives in the village of Balovnoye on Naberezhnaya street. It's nearby Nikolayev. Direct distance is 13 km; distance by roads - 20 km. One-hectare plot with one side access to the Southern Bug River. We can assume they have a small private marina. The location is convenient, because you can easily get to the Black Sea by water, without using land transport to move. Holmes can be right again about transferring the artifacts to Ukraine. Looking at Tyutkin's house location, it was easy for them.

Despite the late time, the place was busy. But the bad thing is, there are no cameras along the street. Or they were, but now they're not working. The closest cameras are far away, on Selikatnaya street. There are many office premises and banks on this street. It's already Nikolayev. There are no CCTV cameras in the village at all. Before reaching the Greenhouse-Vegetable Plant there is a street to the left, which also leads to the city center, but passes Selikatnaya street. They could go in a roundabout way and leave for the Kiev highway. Thus, we checked all the roads that lead from Naberezhnaya Street towards the city center and towards the airport. I could not believe in it. But viewing the recordings from the city video surveillance cameras did not give any results. We spent a lot of time and it was all for nothing. But Holmes was not discouraged. This, on the contrary, encouraged him to dig deeper.

- Do you think we can find a tractor and a truck?
- Of course. How else? They cannot fly to space. Although it's impossible to deny the option of a helicopter. It's expensive. I can admit it's reliable. If they took this option, then the chances of finding the criminals are tiny.

- But still, the cameras had to record the movement of an empty truck and tractor moving from the side of Naberezhnaya Street.
- Not necessary. I hope you noticed there is the Greenhouse and Vegetable Plant on the way to the city center. After viewing the recordings from the city's CCTV cameras, I am sure the criminals rented this vehicle at this enterprise. This is a reasonable explanation why they didn't get on the cameras.
- What did Tyutkin store under the pool, and where is the cargo?
- I am sure he stored the statue of Nereid riding on a dolphin under the pool. It's a great hiding place. What about the second part of your question? This is our task to find where the cargo is. The key thing: one part of Tyutkin's section goes to the river. In this case, it would be ridiculous not to have a private marina and a personal boat, or maybe a small frigate. The only catch is — we cannot verify this information while sitting in Kiev. To do this, we need to go to the crime scene and examine everything by ourselves. If there are no traces of a tractor and a lorry on its pier, then it will be necessary to look for another nearby pier. If checking this option does not give a positive result, then only one option remains — the helicopter. Observing the CCTV cameras, I found something interesting. An old silver-colored sedan hit the surveillance cameras just around 4:20 in the afternoon on Cherry Street. When you turn near the Greenhouse and Vegetable Plant, then this street will lead directly to Cherry Street. This street is a detour through which you can get to Nikolayev International Airport. But this sedan no longer was caught on any camera. He seemed to fall through the ground.
- Where could they disappear?
- It's a good question. Let's eat and go to the railway station. Or we can miss the train.

Chapter IV: Journey and investigation under disguise

After dinner, we gathered our stuff for traveling and after half an hour we got into the taxi. We arrived at the station early, and had almost another hour left to our departure. Holmes, as always, immersed himself in working with a computer. According to his stone facial features, it was impossible to read whether his searches were successfully advancing. I just have to watch the people around me and be on the alert in case of danger. Thank God no accidents occurred at the station. We calmly boarded the train. Holmes bought tickets in SV carriage in the second compartment. The coupe is designed for two people. Despite the late hour, the atmosphere in the carriage was quite noisy. It is clear; the summer is the period of vacations. Many people go south to bask in the sun and swim in the warm sea. I have not seen so noisy atmosphere for a long time. Neighbors from the third compartment came to us and offered to join their holiday. It turned out that a group of artists was not going on vacation, but to take part in competitions among youth theaters. Competitions will be held in Ochakovo. We refused, citing tiredness after a hard day. You understand why we did it. Who knows who they really are? It could be professor's persons. We cannot put our life into the danger and to give them an opportunity in fulfilling their dirty plan. It's easy to put poison into the meal or alcohol.

The wagon conductor came to us to check the tickets. She gave to Holmes the letter. It was a mark she is from Mycroft's team. In the letter we got the instruction on what we have to do. In our couchette under the seats, we found two empty bags. We repack our belongings into it. Our bags we left empty. Holmes had two bags. One of them he left without repacking. We were in our way about half an hour when Holmes said:

- At last, I found the fifth person. Tuytkin pronounced in the wrong way his surname, or he said it softly, and no one could understand the right word. He is not Murzya, but Murzyan. He was a sailor who managed the ship. His name was Alexius. Four years ago he was accused of smuggling artifacts from the ships, which were found nearby the island of Cabrera. The judges sentenced him on ten years' imprisonment. Immediately from the court he was transferred to the prison. In some time, he was killed. According to the article, it had happened during the stroll hours. Some convicts argued and began to fight. Alexius was passing by nearby them. The case was closed as a casual murdering, because the detective didn't find any motives for killing Alexius. The convicts didn't know each other. But. There is one "BUT!"
- I don't like your "But", Holmes. It always leads to something awful.
- This time it's very interesting and helpful information. This accident had happened after one year of his imprisonment. Moreover, it had happened after he sent the appeal to the court. We have to find the motive which he showed in this document. I told you, something had happened four years ago with Tyrin's deals and his surroundings.
- Where Murzyan lived?
- He is from Odessa. Alexius had a wife and two children. She is still live in Odessa.
- Where did you find this information? Can we believe in it?
- I checked all photos, which Tyrin's scuba diver showed on the Facebook. There are a few photos with the man from Cyprus and Alexius.

- Professor can destroy this information. Did you copy the photos?
- Sure. One copy I sent to Mycroft's email. The other one I saved in my cloud. I made print screens. If we be lucky, we'll find Murzyan's wife. May he have left something to her for his rescuing. But we can do it only after Tuytkin's and Tyrin's arrest. Otherwise we'll cause a problem for her.
- What now? It's almost midnight.
- O. We have a lot of work to do.

With this words Holmes took his not repacked bag, and opened it. You can guess what it means… Yes. We're going to change our appearance. At 0:37am we got from the wagon at the Korsun railway station. This time we transferred into two women. Thanks to God, there is a style, when it's hard to tell if these clothes were for men or women. We wore the loose flax trousers and silk tunics, which hid our arms. The sandals were made in men's style, and I felt comfortable wearing it. Holmes wore a long brown-haired wig. I had a blond-haired wig, which fitted to my light skin. Also, Holmes made a make-up suitable for our appearance. We left our coupe imperceptibly. The conductor came and asked if we need something. Holmes thanked and answered we are going to bed. During this conversation we took our bags and were ready for departure. Before her coming, we put mannequins into our beds. In such a manner we have simulated our presence. When we stepped on the wagon's corridor, the conductor wished goodnight and closed the coupe. She walked towards the exit. In a few minutes we followed her. The door in the first coupe was open, but no one paid attention on two women, which were intend to leave the wagon.

We found Steve quickly. He was standing nearby Railway Station entrance. Holmes sat at the steer and we set off. In 5 hours we arrived to our destination. Mycroft's person Ruslan was waiting for us in the apartment. He rented the four-rooms apartment on the outskirts of the city.

It is near to the village Balovnoye. We had a brief rest till 9:30am. When we woke up, we found the served table with breakfast. As appeared, there was the refrigerator, full of food. We needed not to go somewhere to have a meal. Mycroft's preparation impressed. During the breakfast Holmes had a call from Mycroft. He switched on the speakerphone:

- Bad news, Holmes. I arranged to put my doctor psychiatrist into the central hospital for replacing the doctor, who took care about Tyutkin Anton. The previous doctor was unhappy with the changes. He complained to Tyutkin's daughter. She arrived at the hospital around 9 in the morning, but could have changed nothing. On the contrary, because of this visit, we put Lydia in the list of suspects.
- What do you suspect her of?
- While she arrived my doctor has already visited the patient. Anton's condition alerted him. He is constantly sleeping or in a state of prostration. His brain is not functioning. After examining his medical record, the doctor concluded: the appearance of his schizophrenia was provoked by medical pills. During the events of three years ago, the patient experienced a great stress. The doctor prescribed to him some drugs for long-term use. These drugs have side effects in the form of hallucinations. According to the instructions for these drugs, if side effects occur, you must stop taking the medicine and consult a doctor. It's difficult to say whether he went to the doctor, since it's useless to speak with him now. But every time, when Anton came to the hospital, the doctor continued to prescribe this medicine in his card. Moreover, in Russia they announced the toxicity of this drug and banned its use in medical practice for two years ago. When the daughter arrived, she immediately turned to the head doctor of the hospital. He was already instructed in what to answer. The fact is, in Nikolayev, like in every city, we have our own people in the city administration. This man called the head doctor and ordered to appoint a new psychiatrist who will treat Tyutkin. This demand impressed the head doctor. He could

not understand our intervention into the treatment process. According to our explanation, it's caring for an enterprising and respected person who has his own business, and pays good taxes to the budget. The head doctor was glad to hear this and obeyed to an order. Lydia had nothing to do as only to retreat.

- It looks like Lydia, the one who needs to keep Tyutkin in a state of somnambulism. Where is she now?

- After the hospital, she drove to the major restaurant. She is there now. It seemed Lydia is intending to go somewhere, because she didn't allow the guard to re-drive her car inside the restaurant yard.

- Is this the bad news which you've mentioned about?

- No. We were following the doctor. After making a call to someone, he was going to leave the hospital. My people prevented him to do it. They arrested him and transferred to our place. According to the outgoing calls of his phone, the last call was to America. This means his boss is in America, and it was he who ordered him to leave the hospital immediately. During interrogation, the doctor asked for water. No signs of trouble. After his arrest, my people checked all his things and found nothing suspicious. When a glass of water was placed in front of him, he took it in his hands. He had handcuffs on his hands. But instead of drinking water, he bit his sleeve. A minute later, the doctor died. He sewed an ampoule of poison into the sleeve.

- It looks like the plan B of the professor Moriarty. Don't you think?

- I am sure about it. He is in America right now. The proof of our assumption is a tattoo on the doctor's wrist. He is from the organization of "Cleaners".

- Analyzing what happened, do you think Lydia joined this organization too?

- Not excluded. But not a fact. Her behavior is really not logical. Why would she keep her father in a state of schizophrenia? Is she so hungry for power?

- Spoiled people find it difficult to wait for their time to enter the legal inheritance. Sometimes rich children "help" their parents quicker leave for another world. Notify if she is planning to go somewhere. After breakfast we are going to go to look for the pier and we need to know how to behave. What about the news of our train?
- You all overslept. The TV broadcasted this news on at 8 in the morning. They will do it again at 10. Turn on the TV. The time for the release of the news portal is coming soon. One more thing, Holmes. After the conversation with the head doctor, Lydia visited her father. When she left, Tyutkin calmed down. He told to the doctor: "Now all will be okay. She will avenge me." I cannot explain to you what it means.

Having finished breakfast, we didn't spend time on watching the news. Instead of it, we divided into two parts, and went to investigate. Steve drove to the Tyutkin's mansion. We with Ruslan went to make an excursion on the river. With aim to find how the statue was transferred from the Tyutkin house, we needed to find the pier. The tour company opened at 10am. We were the first visitors. The owner gladly welcomed us. Our excursion will last two hours. The guide was telling about Nikolayev, and a lot of interesting stories. Ruslan asked guide what we needed. We still were dressed in women's clothes, and could not speak, because of our men's voice. From time to time we wrote on the paper and gave to Ruslan our questions. He introduced us as foreigners, and he was retelling the same story to us on English.

Knowing Lydia was at work, gave to us an opportunity to observe Tyutkin's pier fearlessly. Ruslan asked the guide to stop the boat nearby certain place. For the aim not looked suspicious, he asked the same request almost nearby every pier. The observation of the pier gave to us nothing. To load the statue on the boat, they need the tractor drove on the pier. This pier was thin. It would not bear the heavy transport. I worried. Holmes's eyes reflected the same feelings. If they transferred the goods by helicopter, it will be hard to find them. In this case, any of our attempts will lead to naught.

A little far from we saw the castle. According to guide, this is the last place, which we'll visit in this part of the river. There are no interesting places further on this way. It means this is our last hope. And we found it. The castle complex "River Tale" is visible even from a distance, because it is on a hill and rises beautifully above the river. It is surrounded by a high wall that protected in ancient times from the invasion of enemies. Now this place is open for excursions and weddings and other significant events. The complex has its own pier, to which small vessels and boats moor. This pier differs from all previous ones in its strength. Earlier we met mainly wooden or small piers made of cement. But someone did thoroughly this pier. Its underwater pillars can easily withstand heavyweight. It surprised us, and Ruslan asked about it. According to the guide, this pier was rebuilt less than month ago with the money of a generous benefactor. Now this complex can be visited by small ships and frigates from other coastal cities. Thanks to the modernization of the pier, the number of visitors has increased. And it absolutely did not surprise us, when we heard the name of the benefactor: George Tyrin. Yes. The one Tyrin himself who found Atlantis. And again, Holmes's assumption turned out to be correct. If he paid for the repair of the pier, then clearly he did it for a certain purpose. This is not a small amount of money. And this goal is the second statue of Nereid riding a dolphin. Another question arises: who is his accomplice? Who is the person who knows about the existence of the statue, and can help to steal it? Surely it should be someone from Tyutkin's close surrounding.

The bad thing is that there are no cameras in the pier area. The cameras were in the complex. Now we are sure the criminals sent the statue to Tyrin on the ship using this pier. But how to prove it? They created a good plan: 1) rented equipment at an enterprise located nearby;

2) seizing the moment that nobody was at home, pumped out water from the pool, took the statue and transferred it to the pier; 3) loaded onto a ship and sent to Tyrin. 4) There are no cameras anywhere. There is no evidence of theft. Superb.

The tour of the castle complex was magnificent. I can't say for others, but my thoughts were in search of a statue. After the tour, Ruslan asked for a little time on an independent observation of the complex. The guide could provide us with only twenty minutes, because his boss called to him and notified of the registered next tour. Since the guide left, we could freely do what we needed. Holmes immediately opened his laptop and connected to the cameras of the castle complex. But who knows whether we will find necessary information there. It took ten minutes to download information from all cameras. In this connection, we returned on board the boat earlier than the specified time.

When we returned to our apartments, Steve was already there. He also downloaded information from cameras installed in Tyutkin's mansion and at nearby neighbors. Again the boring hours of watching CCTV cameras stretched. This time there were four of us, and the work went faster. We were lucky. Although Tyutkin's cells were empty, his neighbors' cameras recorded a taxi which arrived at Tyutkin's house about a month ago. There were two passengers in the car. But it was possible to consider only one who was sitting next to the driver. It was a man. Holmes checked the man's photo for resemblance to the divers who escaped from a psychiatric hospital. The program confirmed the similarity. It was Taras Avdeev. Whether Tyutkin let them into the house is not known. One fact is obvious: after their visit, Tyutkin was scared in earnest and decided to take the jewelry from the bank home. Although where is the logic? To keep artifacts in the bank is safer than at home. Or did he have the other plan? Holmes contacted to Mycroft. He told what we found and asked for help. We needed the confirmation: did Tyutkin meet scuba divers or not? And why after their meeting he decided to take the ancient artifacts from the bank? In some time, Mycroft called back. The questions stayed opened. Anton remembered nothing. He needs more time for recovering.

Back to the surveillance cameras. One chamber of the castle complex recorded how a tractor and an onboard ZIL drove up to the pier. It was not at night, but at 8:30pm. Transport numbers were visible. This will facilitate further searches. As it turned out, Mycroft sent to Nikolayev not two people, a doctor and Ruslan, but the entire group. Two of them took the doctor for interrogation. We have sent the rest part of the representatives of this group to search for the tractor and an onboard ZIL.

The second camera, which was installed in the pier's direction, was recording people on board of a small frigate. One of them was none other than Tyrin himself. The circle is closed. It remains to find out the name of the traitor from Tyutkin's entourage. It goes without saying that the drivers of the tractor and the truck could not hand over the goods themselves. Someone else should have been present. Before loading the goods, Tyrin got off the ship and walked towards the castle. Who he was talking to was not visible. No other cars at that time approached the pier from the side of Tyutkin's house. Holmes checked the recordings of other cameras that are directed towards the road, which went to the International Airport. In a short time, he said:

■ At last. I caught him. According to one camera's recording, a cool racing-type foreign car drove up to the castle complex ten minutes before the arrival of the truck and the tractor. The state number is clearly visible. I'll identify the owner by numbers. Okay. Here we go. — In a few minutes he said with a great surprise. — What's this?
■ What's up? — We asked in unison.
■ It's Lydia Tyutkin's car.

- How can it be? — I came to his desk and looked at the display. Steve and Ruslan did the same. — It's really her car. Listen. Can someone steal or ask to drive her car and meanwhile to do this robbery?
- We need to check it.
- But how will you do it? Where is the logic in her behavior? — I continued conversation. — We suspect Lydia in keeping her father in the status of schizophrenia. Now we saw her working together with Tyrin. Which game does she play?
- Who knows? Watson. It's what we have to find out.

The ring of Holmes's telephone interrupted our conversation. It was Mycroft. In the same time, we heard the beep of his telephone, which announced of receiving the message. Holmes turned on the speakerphone:

- Lydia left the city. She is driving towards Odessa.
- Good. One of cameras from the castle complex "River Tale" recorded her car when Tyrin was loading the statue on his ship. We need to check it was Lydia, or someone used her car.
- That's interesting. I'll ask to check cameras in the hospital. According to her words, she was with the father till the late evening. Be in touch.

Holmes hung up. While the message was opening for reading, he announced:

- It's about Lydia's correspondents. — With these words he stood still.

A few minutes we were waiting for what he will read. But Holmes kept silence. Only his face changed. It became a little pale.

- What's going on? — I interrupted the annoying silence.
- Tyrin is in danger. What time is it? — He looked at his watch. — It's 3:05pm. We have to hurry!
- Why did you conclude Tyrin is in danger? Where are we going?

Chapter V: How to find the door to the bunker?

Seemed Holmes didn't to hear my question. He already called someone. And his respondent picked up the phone. It was Mycroft. Holmes switched on the speakerphone:

- Do you have a group of marines in Odessa?
- Sure. What's the matter?
- Lydia is going to kill Tyrin. Send them to his house. My friend restored deleted information in her phone. According to the correspondence between Lydia and her American acquaintance, he found out about her family's harm, which occurred three years ago, and promised to help her avenge. In addition, if she gives him the jewelry that her father kept in the bank, she will receive the compensation for the damage in millions of dollars. Lydia agreed with the professor to sell the statue at auction, and after then she would kill Tyrin. They have put on the auction only head of statue in case don't draw unnecessary attention. In reality they plan to sell the entire statue. She cannot kill him until they complete the sale. But as soon as the bets are closed, and the statue is sold, she will kill George. And instead of Tyrin's data, Lydia will send her data to where to transfer the money. The auction starts at five in the evening. We need the marines, because it's more likely that she will ship the statue by sea. This is the most convenient way, since Tyrin lives on the seashore and he has his own pier for mooring ships. And

so it's safer. No one will pay attention to what is on the ship. We also go to Odessa.

■ Good. About Lydia. She returned from London at 4pm. After the call from the driver about an accident, she went straight to the hospital. Lydia left hospital at about 6pm.

After listening to this conversation, we understood all. Gathering the necessary stuff with us, we set off to Odessa in a hurry. Ruslan called to his teammates. They agreed to meet in the appointed place nearby the exit of Nikolayev city. Also, the representatives of Ruslan's group found the information about the tractor and an onboard ZIL. These transport vehicles Lydia Tyutkin rented in the Greenhouse and Vegetable Plant. She paid for service by herself.

Holmes drove Steve's car. Steve was sitting nearby Holmes. I sat in the backseat. Almost all the way we kept silence. Holmes was focused on driving. We drove fast enough. Steve car is dark green BMW. It's a new model and fast enough. At those intervals of the road where there were no settlements and traffic rules allowed, Holmes squeezed out of the car all that she could provide. As a result, at a quarter to five, or after one hour and thirty minutes, we drove into the glorious City of Odessa. Since Tyrin lives in the Kiev region of Odessa on Vasily Simonenko Street, we must drive through the entire city. But it was not so simple. Many organizations work up to 5pm. Some people were driving to the beaches, which are in the city center. In short, from time to time we got stuck in traffic jams. The same fate befell the Mycroft's group. Since Ruslan stopped to pick up his people, we arrived first to our destination. A trip through the city took us almost forty-five minutes.

Tyrin's mansion was more like a miniature palace than a pensioner's usual living quarters. According to Holmes, Tyrin lives off the state. Since he was the ambassador of Ukraine, the state pays all utility bills instead. So interesting. True? The smuggler who robbed the state budget is held in high esteem and has such significant privileges. When we arrived at the gate, there were already some onlookers curious about what was happening at their neighbors. But it could be just passers-by, who drew attention to a group of military men heading for the house. A military man met us nearby at the gate. Holmes showed the documents, and the man allowed to us to go into the courtyard. The house was a little off the gate. There was a cobblestone path leading to the house, on both sides, lined with stunted roses. Paths forked around the perimeter of the entire courtyard. The land area is enormous, perhaps about a hectare. Around you can see well-groomed flower beds and fruit trees undersized.

In all this, only one thing was incomprehensible: why did the military scurry about madly back and forth as if they had lost something important and could not find it. When we entered the house, the leader of the group met us. He introduced himself as captain Gruzdev Konstantin. He was of medium height with a well-built figure. For the first few seconds he looked curiously at Holmes. Probably the man on duty at the gate announced our arrival. We greeted each other. Holmes asked about the turmoil we observed.

■ Our people watched Lydia from her entrance to Odessa through city CCTV cameras. She arrived here at five minutes to five. At this time, our boats were near to Tyrin's pier without attracting attention. According to our data, the sale of the statue of Nereid riding on a dolphin will be sold third. In this regard, we scheduled the beginning of the operation for 5:10pm. At the showed time, we were on the pier and silently approached to the house. The door of the house was open. We searched the entire house but found no one. We determined with special equipment that a bunker is in the basement. But we still have not found where the entrance of this bunker. Lydia entered the house. It's for sure. From the defined street, our man followed her by a motorcycle. There are no cameras in this area and even near Tyrin's house.

- Odessa stands on the catacombs. They could hide using a secret passage.
- Maybe you are right.
- What about the statue?
- There is a hangar nearby the house. A small ship can easily fit inside it. In addition, the rail tracks run from the pier to the hangar. I think Tyrin put his ship in the hangar for the winter. The statue stands in this hangar.
- Good. Let's look for the entrance to the bunker.

Holmes rushed around the house and returned to the courtyard. Soon Ruslan's group arrived and joined to the search. It obvious Konstantin notified Ruslan about the problem by phone, because immediately upon arrival he got into work without asking unnecessary questions. In the hangar, nothing attracted Holmes's attention. There really was the statue. Its weight is about 200 kilograms. The color of the statue surprised me. It is like yellow gold, but shone much brighter. In the sun, it looks like a fiery sparkle. Unbelievable. Holmes contemplated the statue for several minutes and then completely lost interest in it. At this pace, we went almost to the exit of the estate to the pier. Near to the exit stood a monument to the helm of a ship made of wood using stones. It's difficult to say how precious they are. Holmes examined the helm and headed for the pier. Looking at this pier, I can tell you with confidence that anyone can envy Tyrin. He built the pier in a great way. Any ships can easily moor to it, except for the large ones. The platform is made of a durable material that can withstand any heavy equipment. In addition, he installed a crane near the pier which allows you to unload the ship without entering the pier. Holmes inspected the pier and returned to the estate. On the way back, he again stopped near the monument of the helm.

- What are you looking at? — I asked.
- Look at this monument. Don't you consider strange to create the monument for helm between the house and pier? It can be a key.
- Surely it's weird, but it located too far from the house. Don't you think?
- Let's check. — He called to someone. The respondent took the call. — Ruslan. Tell your men to leave the house. Maybe I found the key to the bunker.

He tried to turn the helm, but nothing worked. While he was busy with the helm, Ruslan and Konstantin came to us. There was a drawing in the central part of the helm. People, from the organization "Cleaners", have on their wrists the same picture in the form of a tattoo. It looked like the picture was drawn recently. Maybe it's a hint. Holmes pressed the middle part of the helm and also without result. He began to study every inch of the helm. None of the parts was the key to opening the bunker.

- I think you should admit, you were mistaken. — Konstantin told Holmes. I felt proud note in his voice.

But Holmes was so absorbed in his thoughts that he hardly heard comments.

- We can blow up part of the floor. The floor of the house is not wooden, but concrete. This is the only solution to get inside the bunker. There are cameras in the house and in the courtyard. Surely the criminals saw our presence and had a lot of time to hide. We need to act. We are already late.

Konstantin wanted to say something else, but at this time Holmes stood at the helm and pulled it towards himself. And it worked. Holmes turned to us and said:

- We haven't been late. My man informed me recently that, for some reason, the sale of the statue was moved to the end of the line. The auction will last one hour. Now we have five minutes to six. Right now, there is a sale of a statue of Nereid riding on a dolphin.

Suddenly we heard the cries of the military. The entrance to the bunker has opened.

Chapter VI: Inglorious death of the smuggler

We rushed to the house. As it turned out, the entrance to the bunker was straight in the lobby at the entrance to the house. When Holmes pulled the helm toward himself, part of the floor sank lower and, with the help of a slide, drove under the floor, freeing the passage into the bunker. Since the floor in the lobby was made of tiles, it was difficult to determine that a special mechanism was installed under the floor. When we entered the house, Ruslan's team was working on a laser alarm. Tyrin built his shelter with all the precautions. He updated the alarm methods as new emerging technologies emerged. At last, the alarm was turning off, and we went there. The situation in the bunker was not less stunning. The terrifying picture appeared before us. Bloodied Lydia stood nailed to the wall with a spear. A revolver lay near her. After the inspecting the revolver, we could assume that Lydia made one shot. It was hard to say whether she wounded Tyrin. He escaped. The bunker was made in the form of a circle. Across its perimeter, we saw peaks of spears inside the walls. It's obvious, Tyrin installed somewhere a mechanism, with which help he can shoot a spear at the desired object. It was necessary to move carefully so as not to fall under the "crazy" bullet. In such a place, you can easily expect a trick in the form of a shot from somewhere. Perhaps Tyrin set up something else, except the spears, in this room for protection. Answer on this question we can have after a thorough inspection and study of the entire bunker. But now there is no time for this. We need to find Tyrin, who took advantage of the underpass and disappeared. Or maybe a catacomb branch runs under his house. Which is also very likely. The task seems to be understandable, but as Holmes says: there is one "But". To tell the truth, I don't like this "But". Currently we ended up in the room which contains surprises. We need to find the right button or lever to open the door to the underpass. At the same time, we have to avoid causing the shot from the spear or some other weapon.

Holmes sat down at the computer and started working. Soon, he turned off all the secrets of this room, and we could freely move around the bunker. Finding the door from here was not a simple task. It can be anywhere. To avoid hurting someone from the teams, Holmes asked everyone to leave this place. He allowed to stay with him only me. I thought the exit would be somewhere in the wall. But in the reality, we faced another surprise. Holmes continued to work with the computer. In some time, he clicked by the mouse on something on the screen, and part of the bunker floor rose. A spiral staircase appeared before our eyes, going deep underground. In the same time, we heard the sounds of breaking windows and of falling down something heavy accompanied with explosion. It looked like a slight earthquake.

■ It's like in the book of the famous science fiction writer Jules Verne's "Journey to the Center of the Earth". — Holmes joked.

But somehow no one reacted to his joke. Or maybe it was not a joke?

■ What's the sound? — I asked — From where did it come?

We looked at each other's, but no one could give the answer on my question. The mansion's windows crashed. Konstantin sent his subordinates to check outside. We were going to verify the underground passage. There was a set of flashlights in the bunker. We armed with them and began to descend underground. Holmes went first. I followed him.

Next went Ruslan. The representatives of his group followed him. Konstantin's group stayed to guard the mansion and to find out what had happened outside. The descent was quite deep, about fifty meters. Then we got into the catacombs. Yes. The city of Odessa is known for its catacombs. Today, not all of them have been investigated. When we appeared in the catacombs, it was necessary to decide which way to go. After examining the walls, Holmes suggested going right. According to his examination, the walls on the right side looked more worn, while on the opposite side they were absolutely untouched. We moved in a normal step, because the road was smooth. Soon the road began to rise markedly. By the time it was possible to determine that, we walked about two kilometers. Ahead, the road narrowed, and we had to walk one after another. Ten minutes later we were in front of the door. The door was ajar. We heard the cars noise and human voices. When we went outside, bright sunlight blinded us. It was hard to watch for several minutes. In a short time, the eyes got used to sunshine, and we could look around where we appeared. The door from the catacombs led us to the basement of the living building, from which we got into the entrance and into the courtyard. Before us we saw a crowd of people and heard an approaching sound of an ambulance siren. Holmes walked toward the crowd. I thought someone felt bad, and passers-by called an ambulance. But it turned out quite differently. Another surprise awaited us at the street: on the ground lay a man on his face. Someone shot him from his back into his head. The bullet went right through. He was dead. A policeman was bustling next to a corpse. Holmes introduced himself to the policeman, and the last politely allowed to examine the victim. Much to our surprise, it was none other than Tyrin. His personality was identified quickly, because he had an international passport with him.

You can say: what an irony of fate? He killed Lydia in his bunker. According to examination, he had no the other wound. It means Lydia fired at him, but didn't hit him. And someone killed him on the street.

Who did this? Who is the killer? Someone had to know that Tyrin will go this way. He had not only a passport but also bank cards of both Ukrainian and foreign banks. Looking at the presence of bank cards of foreign banks, he does not quite look like a ruined person. Did Tyrin create for himself such an image, so that no one would guess about his countless treasures? Maybe so. This will be clear after checking all of his bank accounts. Now the question number one is: who killed him? Second - from where did they shoot? Observing the location of the corpse, Holmes determined where they were shooting from. Ruslan's group went to check on the building.

We went examining the yard. The courtyard itself is like a square well. After exiting the porch, a person enters the yard. This happens with three more houses. On the one hand, such a yard is convenient for mothers with children. A playground has been built in the middle of it. There are benches around the playground. But on the other hand, there are no CCTV cameras in residential buildings. And this complicates the investigation process. In order to get to the city transport, you need to go out from the entrance, go along the house, turn right. Then you'll see the transport stop. The criminal killed Tyrin when he went to the exit from the courtyard. Horrible death. We also didn't find CCTV cameras at the road. This part of the city is far from the center. And in the very center of Odessa there are not many cameras. Unless we could use the cameras of banks. But on this part of the street there were no office premises. This is a classic sleeping area.

- Who do you think killed him? — I asked Holmes.
- It's the work of the professor Moriarty.
- What is your assumption based on?
- Think yourself. Lydia was negotiating with someone from America. He promised to her she will avenge her father. It's an incontrovertible fact that professor Moriarty is now in America. If we assume Moriarty was behind Tyrin, this explains why he could trade artifacts on the

black market and even at open auctions. But something went wrong. There must have been a conflict between them. As a result, George retired. Why didn't the professor kill Tyrin before? That's the question. Perhaps he knew valuable information, which the professor was interesting in.

- What has changed now? Do you think Tyrin discovered his secret to Moriarty, and the professor killed him?
- Who knows? In my opinion, the professor was afraid of letting this information fall into our hands.
- But no one knows we're alive.
- You are so naïve. Does the person who always has plan B in reserve, don't know that his agents were arrested on the train? It's nonsense. I, Watson, are alarmed by something else. Where is Tyrin's phone? I didn't find it when I examined the body. There was no the telephone in the things that the policeman provided us for inspection.
- Do you think someone stole the telephone?
- There are several options here. It's hard to say which one is right. — Holmes called to someone while continuing to talk with me. — The best option for us if he forgot his phone in the bunker. Tyrin left his shelter in a hurry. In such a situation, it's possible. — Holmes's respondent picked up the phone. — Konstantin. Didn't you find Tyrin's phone in the bunker? ...... Really? It's great. We'll arrive soon. — The Holmes hung up. — We are lucky. Tyrin forgot the phone at home.

Soon Holmes received a notification from Ruslan that their investigation was also without result. During a survey of the building, it was determined that an unknown middle-aged man signed a rental contract for the premises a week ago. By all signs and behavior, he looked like an ordinary vacationer. In the morning and evening he went to the beach. He ate in a cafe which is a block from the house. Ruslan interviewed tenants and the landlord. But they could not give any special comments. Already in a cafe, he was described in more detail. He liked one waitress, and they had a brief affair. According to her description, we concluded that it was Kravets. Yes. The same Kravets, who is the sniper of the professor Moriarty. Holmes's assumption turned out to be correct.

Chapter VII: Revenge as an easy method of human manipulation

W e had no choice but to return to Tyrin's mansion and continue to examine his estate and bank accounts. We came back using a taxi. You could get there by public transport, but it would take a lot of time. Under the ground we walked three kilometers or so. Unfortunately, there is no such direct road on the earth's surface. We caught a taxi and after ten minutes were already in place.

Konstantin met us with bad news. He found an explanation for the sound of the fall of something heavy, accompanied by an explosion and a slight wobble of the earth. The statue of Nereid riding on a dolphin fell underground and exploded there. We went to the hangar. An enormous pit gaped at the site of the statue. It was hard to estimate how deep the pit was. The specialists will check. It's so pity that the statue was destroyed.

- How could this happen? — I asked Holmes.
- I think Tyrin suspected Lydia of her intention to avenge her father. Perhaps someone predetermined it.
- You want to say that there is a traitor among the professor's surrounding?
- Not excluded. Moriarty's business is built on lies, setbacks and robbery. You can long list in what frauds and scams he took part. You yourself saw how he tried to take over businesses in the different

regions of Ukraine. Because of using such methods, there are the victims who want to avenge their fall or ruin. It's obvious. But there may be another option. Tyrin bribed an informant who regularly notified him of the professor's actions or plans. For this he paid the informant good money. It's unnecessary to speculate now which option is the right one. The important thing is, he knew about Lydia's plan and was ready for it. It's easy to guess, if we are talking about the statue, then the professor is most likely involved in this matter. I note it was the statue's sale that united Tyrin and Lydia together.

■ In my opinion, a third option is feasible: Tyrin wanted to sell the statue and take all the money for himself.

■ This is out of the question, Watson. If he considered only this option, he would not allow the statue to go underground. What prevented him from hiring an assassin and to kill Lydia in Nikolayev straight after the loading the statue on his ship? Nothing. But he did not do it. Today is Thursday. He got the statue on Monday.

■ Persuasively.

■ You cannot object that Tyrin saw a group of marines surrounding his house. Surely, it concerned him. Lydia had to wait for the end of the auction to fill out a form where to transfer money instead of Tyrin. Until that moment, she could not kill him. And then next problem occurred. Lydia learned that the sale of the statue was moved to the very end of the line. It was out of her plans. She is eccentric and nervous woman. In a fit of anger that everything is not going according to her plan, she tried to kill Tyrin. But in response, he, with one click of the mouse, releases a spear at her. Analyzing the entire story, I think it was Tyrin, who postponed the sale of the statue to the end of the line. I assume he ordered to create the special program for him. According to this program, in case if someone opened the exit from the bunker, except him, the statue will fall underground. Even if we were not here, and Lydia still managed to kill him, she could not have taken the statue. He has a fairly modernized bunker. And it's easy to do.

■ Your words make sense. But what now?

■ We need to check Tyrin's phone and to see how the auction went. Although I am confident that the statue was not sold. Tyrin left the bunker before the scheduled time for sale. Still, we need to check with whom he contacted. Maybe we'll find the organizer of this auction. In addition, his bank cards can also give us valuable information.

We went to the bunker. Lydia was not there. The police took her corpse to the morgue for making the autopsy. Konstantin with his group left. They have no what to do here. Because Ruslan's team specialized in such cases, they continued the investigation with us. Also, Ruslan called to the police. Holmes started to work from checking Tyrin's telephone. In a few minutes, he smiled and said:

■ It was not the informant who warned Tyrin about danger. He got the message on Tuesday evening from the same American telephone number as Lydia had. Look.

This is the text of warning: "Be aware. Lydia plans to kill you. I am on your side. Trust me."

■ If this is Moriarty, he plays a dirty game. — I said. — What was in the messages, which Lydia received from the American number?

Holmes took his phone out of his pocket and showed me Lydia's correspondence with the American respondent. It took place 12th July 2010. This is the correspondence itself:

■ "I can help your dream come true. For many years you have been waiting for the moment to avenge the incident of three years ago, which brought your family so much sorrow.

■ Who you are?

- Your father and I were business partners.
- I know all the people from his business, since I have been doing it myself for three years. But I have heard nothing about you. What is your name?
- If your father didn't tell you my name, it means for you it doesn't matter. Your father was kind and always helped to me. I don't want to look ungrateful. Because of this, I can no longer keep silence about what had happened over him. The feelings of injustice gnaw at me constantly.
- Do you know who ordered the robbery in our house?
- Sure.
- You were silent for three years. So why should I believe you now?
- I had reasons for this. Now I can help you.
- What is your help?
- I can help you deal with the customer of the tragedy of your family.
- Who is he?
- Tyrin.
- I know it. And what?
- After retiring, Tyrin was mired in gambling and squandered his entire fortune in a year. He had nothing to live on. His sculpture of Nereid, riding on a dolphin, was sold four and a half years ago at an auction in London. The deal from the second sculpture, the head of a flying horse, belonged to Tyrin and your father in half. They sold it in Odessa in your father's gallery. Only Tyrin knew about the existence of the second sculpture of Nereid, and that it was in your home. You called to the police, and this prevented them to take out the sculpture. After this event, your father ordered the construction of a pool in your mansion. He has hidden a sculpture under the bottom of the pool.
- How did you find out about this? The sculpture was really in the house before the incident three years ago. After that, we hid her under the pool, and no one knew about it.

- You're wrong. Your father is very naïve. He himself told Tyrin about this. He could not even imagine that it was Tyrin who was the organizer of your tragedy.
- My father knew about Tyrin. He could not tell to him this information.
- I have my informants. Your father is sick, and he did it. It's the truth, as it is. I found out about the rest of the story recently. This is another reason I contacted you after three years. Three years ago, your father told me in detail about what happened. According to his description, everything looked like an ordinary robbery. The thieves didn't steal any values. They didn't reach the room where the statue stood. Or maybe they didn't know where it was. After that, your father put all the artifacts in the bank. It was more reliable. He did this about my advice.
- What revenge plan can you offer?
- Offer Tyrin to auction the sculpture of Nereid. After the sale, you can kill him. But be careful. You need to kill him before sending data to the site where to transfer the money. If you don't, the money will be sent to two accounts. After that, you cannot pick them up. He has opened accounts with foreign banks, which he uses for this kind of receipt of money.
- Why should I sell sculpture? Only to kill Tyrin?
- Do you want to revenge? Or maybe you don't need money?
- But what do you want in return? I don't think it's all for free.
- I want to buy the artifacts, which your father holds in a bank. With my help, you will get the permission of the National Bank to open a foreign currency account in the offshore. I'll transfer the money there. Since no one finds out about the sale, you need not to pay the taxes. Net profit.
- The jewelry is always better than money. They are more liquid.
- This is so, if the jewelry was acquired by legal means. You know well how your father has got these artifacts. It's the result of his joined with Tyrin illegal research of the deep of the Mediterranean Sea. Am I

wrong? Where can you sell them? Even if you do this, the police immediately arrest you for hiding the artifacts.

- I need to think.
- A wise decision. Just don't think for a long time.
- Are you threatening me?
- In no case. It's just a friend's warning. The fact is, now auctions are not held so often. It happens about once every half a year. In the past, they used to be held almost every month. There are not many artifacts left that people can offer for sale. I heard the next an auction will hold in Turkey on August 19 at 5pm.
- I understood. If so, I'll touch with you in a week."

In a week, 19th July, the next correspondence occurred. Here it is:

- "I am ready to have a deal with you, but I don't know how to take the artifacts from the bank. Only my father has the access to the bank cell.
- This is not a problem. If you change his medicine, you'll can convince him to take the jewelry from the bank.
- I am not a doctor. How can I change something? I don't want to harm him.
- You'll not harm him. Just buy the same medicine with a higher dose. That's all what you need to do. He will have hallucinations. It is easy to cope with them by cleaning the body with special droppers. He will be put on his feet in two weeks.
- Good. I will do so. What's next? What is your plan? How to take the statue so that my father does not notice, and how to convey the artifacts to you? When are you going to pay for them?
- In two weeks after increasing the dose of the medicine, you can freely talk with your father about the return of the jewelry to your home safe. The conversation must begin from far away. Then you have gradually to increase the pressure in the form of a conviction of the neediness of these actions. Within a week, he should set a date when he will go to

the bank. If you want to avoid falling under the suspicious, you should be abroad on a business trip. It will be better if you leave the country on the eve of the designated day. But you must return home in this particular day. I'll send my people to stage a robbery. No harm will be done to your father. I cannot guaranty the same for his driver. You will have to compensate him, because it will happen when he will be on his duty. His injuries won't be big either. I assure you. Your father will be taken to the hospital. It would be nice if you came back at this time. From the airport you go straight to the hospital. Let's appoint the meeting at 7 pm at your house. You have to rent transport. We will pump out water from the pool. A tractor will dig the pool deeper. Using the crane, we will pick up the statue. A truck will take her to the pier.

- We cannot load a statue onto the ship from our pier. It cannot withstand a truck or a crane.

- Do not worry. You can solve this issue with Tyrin's help. Intrigue him by your plan for the sale of the statue and complain that there is no normal pier. The castle complex "River Tale" is nearby your house. Invite him to repair their pier. For this, you will give him 5 percent of the value of the statue.

- Why should I give him something?

- You will kill him anyway. What do you care what to say? You need to interest him so he deeply swallows the bait and can no longer jump off the hook.

- Okay. I got you. What's next?

- After this, the only details will remain. You will go to his mansion to attend the auction.

- But what if he deceives me and sells the sculpture himself to someone else?

- This is out of the question. In your country, no one will buy it, because the statue is very expensive. If you want to sell such an artifact in Ukraine, cut the price by three quarters. He is too greedy to make such a sacrifice. It is foolish to miss the opportunity to earn more money if they float into your hands by themselves.

■ That is yes. What about paying for the jewelry?

■ To answer on your question, I need a list of jewelry that is in the bank cell. According to this list, we can determine how much they cost. Only after this I can tell when I will pay you.

■ But where can I get this list?

■ Surely your father keeps this list in a safe. Is this a problem for you to check the safe in your house?

■ Not. I'll do it.

■ But that's not all. Send on my email copy of your documents: passport, code. I'll give a request to the National Bank for a license to permit the placement of foreign currency funds in foreign banks. The bank will issue the license within five days. Then I'll help you open the accounts. While the specialists will carry the valuation of the artifacts out, you will open the accounts. And then everything is simple: I am ready to pay you 50 percent of the amount that will be stated in the valuation report. The remaining 50 percent I'll transfer to you when my people will report to me they took the jewelry from your father.

■ How can I believe that you don't deceive me, and you will pay the remaining 50 percent according to the valuation report?

■ How can I believe that you will not deceive me, and on appointed day your father will really take the artifacts from the bank and will drive home alone without his guards and the escorts from the police?

■ It's a logical. We are both at risk. Agreed, then.

■ No wonder there is a proverb: who does not take risks, he does not drink champagne.

■ That's for sure."

The correspondence continued a week later. It was 26th July. Here is its content:

- "The specialists completed the valuation of the jewelry. Their total cost amounted to 10 billion dollars. I transferred money in the amount of 50 percent of the mentioned above sum to your account.
- I confirm receiving the money. Thank you."

On August 7, Lydia sent the next correspondence:

- "My father will go to the bank 16 August around 3pm."
- "Good. Thank you."

On Tuesday morning, August 17, Lydia received the last message:

- "I would be grateful if you would invite to investigate the case of the robbery of your father, the famous detective from Kiev, Sherlock Holmes. This will further confirm your non-involvement in the incident with your father."

Lydia wrote the answer only in the late afternoon at about 6 o'clock:
- "I think I cannot do what you ask. I heard he didn't lose a single case. Why should I put myself into the danger? Do you want to send me to jail?
- He will not reach you. Believe me. I fed up with Holmes and plan to kill him. He gets under my feet and interferes with my work. It's difficult to arrange such event in Kiev. But on the way to you, it will be just right.
- Okay."

After reading the correspondence, I felt the disgusting towards Lydia. I argued with Holmes and defended her. But he appeared right. At first glance, you can't say that a person is obsessed with strong hatred. Many psychologists don't recommend deciding in a fit of anger or in a state of joy. According to their reasoning, in such cases, a person cannot decide deliberately. But Lydia pondered this decision for a week. Whoever tells me that proverbs are not taken from life, I will not believe it. Who came up with the proverb: you will chase two hares, you will not catch a single one? Doesn't it fit to our story? Lydia wanted to kill Tyrin and to get the money from selling the artifacts without paying taxes. Instead of making revenge, she died herself. This is incomprehensible for me. Holmes was tinkering with the auction's site. But I dared to have a conversation with him.

- Lydia died such a stupid death. For what? Don't you think so?
- I agree with you. But no one canceled the God's laws. And people who have received power and money often forget about the simplest commandments.
- What are you talking about?
- The Holy Scripture says: "Vengeance is mine, I will repay, said the Lord." If a person himself decided to avenge the offense inflicted on him, then he deprives God of the privilege that belongs only to Him. God punishes for this.
- It's easy to say when you have experienced nothing like it. There are many situations in life that you want to kill your enemy. But you keep this desire within you, because you will become a killer. And instead of revenge, you will go to jail.
- If you direct your rebuke at me, then you, Watson, are wrong. My parents died twenty years ago. Do you think I was not burning revenge? It burned me severally. If God did not help to me, then it would be impossible to endure this pain. This is the only case that I have not solved. I spoke with an Orthodox priest. He explained to me how to react if I planned something to do, but faced the dead end, and could not fulfill it. There are two options. First, this is not for you and you don't need it. Second, this is not the right time. If you pray to God, He will show you later why it had happened. Surely if He considers you need to know this. After this conversation, I analyzed my events and I understood: what had happened to me, thanks to God's providence, it was better than if I have achieved what I've desired. If I fulfilled some

of my ideas, I could have got in a great trouble. That's why I think the time for the investigation of my parents' case has not come yet. About Lydia. I sincerely feel sorry for her. But she made her choice and paid for it. This deal was initially too risky for her. This behavior reveals her painful self-confidence. Bandits go to business, trusting each other. The killers are hired for money, but they also trusted those who hired them. I cannot tell you they trust to their dealer too much. But still, we can name this as the trust. Lydia made a deal with a person whom she had never seen. Why? Explain me. Usually such people are named either risky or reckless. You can name them whatever you like, but they don't live long, at least in the nature. It's from the practice, Watson.

I didn't answer, because I had no what to say back to Holmes. When we were working with Tyrin's and Lydia's telephones, the police detective arrived. It was the same person responsible for the investigation of Tyrin's death. His name was Bogdan Semchenko. He immediately recognized us. We gave to him the total information about this case. He turned out to be smart. Bogdan was about thirty-five, slim with curious eyes. He had a freckled face. Curly red hair did not at all correspond to his rank. But the choice of the profession doesn't depend on our appearance. Bogdan began his own examination of the entire house, including the bunker.

Chapter VIII: Stunning result of the expertise

After finishing telephones' examination, Holmes returned to his work with the computer. While examining the body of Tyrin, he photographed all the things he found. And now he was checking the information. According to Holmes's research, Tyrin had opened the accounts in many banks in offshore zones. It's one of the way of the criminals for hiding their funds from taxation. Today, his accounts in foreign banks were about five hundred million US dollars. Holmes got the access to Tyrin's banks and made the printouts of bank statements which gave a lot of information for processing. Then he sent the bank statements to Mycroft for the further investigation. I presume it will last long.

In fact, Holmes' assumption about the today's sale of the statue turned out to be true. Tyrin canceled the sale. It was not possible to establish the venue of the auction, because it was virtual. According to the IP address, its founder is in Turkey. The auction was conducted over the Internet remotely. For this aim, the criminals created a special site. Entrance to the site is password protected. Only the bidders could receive the passwords.

Holmes hacked into the site. We found a lot of videos about the auctions, but all participants used sobriquets instead of their names. This confused all of us. How to find a person by sobriquet, which he used only for visiting this club? There was a frequent occurrence that the same people took part in the auction. We paid attention to one man. He took part almost in all auctions. Besides, he had weird sobriquet — Brazilian wanderer. In the nature there is the creature with almost the same name — the Brazilian wandering spider. It belongs to the genus of spiders in the runner family. This genus considers as the most venomous. I remembered about them, because in this year the Brazilian wandering spider was listed in the Guinness Book of Records for their unique and the most dangerous poison.

When Holmes checked to whom Tyrin sold his artifacts, our interest to this man has increased. As we know, Tyrin began to trade them being as ambassador to Spain. In this time, the different people bought the artifacts. But after his appointment as ambassador to Cyprus, Brazilian wanderer became his regular customer. He bought all artifacts, which Tyrin displayed for selling. According to Holmes' assumptions, five years ago Tyrin discovered the sunken Atlantis. The found artifacts were very different: from coins, jewelry to other things utensils. All household utensils were made either of transparent glass, which resembles crystal, or of silver and gold. Once Tyrin displayed an enormous head of a horse on sale. And I assure you, this statue was made of orichalcum. After seeing the statue of Nereid, her fiery radiance cannot be confused with anything. The masters made the head of a horse from the same material. At a glance, the weight of the sculpture was about one hundred kilograms. What should be the weight of the sculpture itself? It's hard to even imagine it. Then Tyrin sold the piece of the statue — some creature's wing. Just like the horse's head, the wing was large and had an impressive weight. It was the second largest sculpture sold during that period and also made of orichalcum. Again, if to believe in the discovery of Atlantis, then this wing could be part of the statues of six flying horses, controlled by Poseidon. These two exhibits, the horse's head and part of the wing, exactly correspond to the description by Plato in his dialogue "Critias" about the statues of the temple in Atlantis. These sales happened about four and a half years ago. Another pair of scrolls made of gold appeared on sale. But their size was slightly smaller than an A4 paper sheet. The thickness of the scrolls was approximately five millimeters. After these, only coins and something small from household utensils were put up for sale. But the large exhibits were no longer on display, except the statue of Nereid riding on a dolphin which was sold in London. And one more thing: Tyrin stopped to take part in auctions four years ago.

Holmes found the hidden safe. Tyrin built it into the wall behind the cupboard. The representatives of Konstantin's group checked the entire bunker before our arrival, but did not find it. A reasonable question arises: how could Holmes find the safe while sitting at the computer? It turns out easy if you understand the programming. Tyrin used the latest technology for his safety. There was a program at the computer, which allows you to open something. The entrance to the software was password protected. But it was not a problem for Holmes. In some time, he gained access to the program and in its menu clicked on the "Open" button. After that, we heard a loud click and the contents of one of the compartment of the cabinet with the clinking of breaking dishes fell to the floor. Inside the cupboard we saw the opened door of the safe. It's noteworthy in this compartment of the cabinet there was no transverse partition, as in ordinary cabinets. But no one paid attention to this, since there were tall ceramic vases inside.

The contents of the safe confirmed one more time that Tyrin was not a beggar. He created such an image with the goal of not attracting the wrong attention of thieves and probably those to whom he sold artifacts. He has done everything to be invisible and inaccessible. When the safe opened, a cube-shaped bag appeared before our eyes. The walls of the cube are 60 centimeters. Inside, we discovered countless treasures. I am not afraid of the word. It's like in Robert Louis Stevenson's book

"Treasure Island". We saw a lot of gold coins, coins from the orichalcum, precious stones and necklaces. Everything is even difficult to describe. In the house we found a few ancient amphorae about a meter high, two Chinese tea sets of the Ming era and the clay plates of ancient production. Tyrin used them in everyday life. Is it something like self-affirmation or what? I cannot understand or to explain why a person should use artifacts instead of ordinary kitchen utensils. But unfortunately we will never know about this.

After finding the safe, Holmes immediately called Mycroft and asked for a group of antique appraisers. Fortunately for us, there are two such people from his group in Odessa. About twenty minutes later they arrived and settled in the large room. There they placed their equipment and work quietly.

During the search of the bunker, we found the documents for the purchase of the deep-sea vehicle "Russ" from a Russian manufacturer. Tyrin bought it in September 2003 when he worked as ambassador to Spain. We also found the agreement with the Illichivsk port for renting a space for storing the bathyscaphe. He signed this contract for four years ago.

It was after midnight, and we were still at Tyrin's mansion. When Mycroft sent to us the experts, he also sent a special plane to Odessa to pick up the jewelry. He seemed to have foreseen that the amount would be very significant. The decision is right. Odessa is a magnificent city, people are friendly and cheerful. But banditry is also on the high level. It's better not to take the risk. The armored van, escorted by two vehicles, arrived at about midnight. They were waiting for the end of the examination. It was 1:20 am when the experts announced about completing their work. The result of the estimation stunned us. According to their examination, there were $70 billion worth of antiques in the Tyrin's house and the safe. This is more than the external debt of our state.

Here you have a beggar. In the collection of Tyrin, the experts found stones whose value exceeds all existing specimens in the world. There were those about which we knew only from ancient chronicles.

The artifacts were loaded into an armored van. The Mycroft's team with the escort were ready to drive to the airport, as suddenly we heard the sound of an approaching helicopter. What was it? Will criminals attack us from the sky? Together with the astonishment, my fear raised too. Goosebumps ran down my skin. I looked at Holmes. He was calm, as always. It meant this is not a threat. Then what?

The helicopter landed nearby the pier. Mycroft's men from the van took the bag with treasures and carried it to the helicopter. My curiosity was bursting me, but I forced myself to keep silence. The helicopter took off. We stood observing his departure. Soon he disappeared into the darkness of the night, and we heard only the receding noise of his engine. I presume our mission ended there. We could think about having a rest.

Chapter IX: Unexpected meeting with the death

The armored van with the escort left the mansion. The detective has finished his examination till their departure, but found nothing new. When we left this place, he sealed the house and assigned the security at the gate and in the courtyard. Bogdan offered us to spend the night in a hotel which was nearby this place. Holmes rejected the offer, because his friend ran a rest house. It is on French Boulevard. We were incredibly lucky, because today the vacationers left, and he expected the next group only after tomorrow. So we, together with the group of Ruslan, calmly settled in the rest house. Holmes called to his friend in advance and established an overnight stay for all of us. On our way there I asked Holmes the question, which was bothering me. It was the suitable time, because we drove in Steve's car without strangers.

■ Why such precautions? Was the armored van not enough? Why did Mycroft send the helicopter?
■ He has a reason for that. If a representative of the professor Moriarty is operating in Odessa, you need to be on the alert.

The answer is comprehensive. He can be right. When you faced such an intelligent opponent, you always need to calculate in advance what problems you might encounter in a situation. Soon we arrived to our destination. The supper was waiting for us. Holmes's friend arranged the romantic meal on the seashore under the light of lanterns. The warm August weather contributed to spending time by the sea. Although the sea was fifty meters from us, no one went swimming. Everyone was tired. We had no time to finish our supper when an explosion broke the night's silence. The sound came from about twenty kilometers from us. As one, we jumped up and listened. There was a slight movement of the ground, as if something heavy fell to the ground.

- What's this? — I asked Holmes. — Did someone blow up an armored van?
- No. I don't think so. This sound came from the direction of the airport.

Hearing Holmes's assumption, we quieted down. The air felt thick. There was a growing tension. While Holmes was calling to Mycroft, Ruslan called to his colleagues who came to the Tyrin's mansion in an armored van. Nothing happened to them. They safely reached their base. If everything is okay with them, then the sound came from the airport. What could have happened there? Surely Mycroft could give the answer, but he did not pick up the phone.

- Do you think the professor Moriarty dared to blow up the plane with the jewels? It's drivel. It cannot be. He's too greedy to do it.
- Why not? In a fit of rage, he ordered to kill Tyrin. He is the only person who knows the location of Atlantis. Do you think he will allow the treasury of Ukraine to be replenished with money and improve the country's solvency? I deeply doubt it.
- We can collect the jewelry after exploding. What will he do then?
- Don't talk nonsense. If they place the explosives nearby the jewelry, then instead of jewelry, only no one needs dust will remain there.
- It might still be fine, and this is not a plane.

Holmes didn't have time to answer as his phone rang. It was Mycroft. Our eyes were on Holmes. Seemed he somehow slouched a little under the weight of what he heard. His features became sharper. He was laconic:

■ What? .... It's bad .... I see .... Order for me the recordings from airport cameras. It has to be ready when we came..... I doubt this is a coincidence. There is a traitor among your men. Check it..... Sure..... Good. We're leaving. — He hung up and turned towards us. His face was pale. — The aircraft has exploded. We must find what's happened.

■ Do my team also under suspect? — Ruslan asked.

■ Give me the telephone numbers, all of your men.

Ruslan gave what Holmes demanded, and we set off. During our way to the airport, Holmes delegated to his friend checking with whom Ruslan's team were connecting during this night. But they turned to be clean. Thank God, we can rely on them. The Odessa International Airport is located just seven kilometers southwest of the city center. We quickly arrived at our destination. When approaching the airport, we saw fire trucks and ambulances. The airport was full of police officers. The commotion felt everywhere. Fear froze on people's faces. I saw the women with eyes red from tears keeping sleepy children in their hands. The airport authorities canceled the nearest flights. There was turmoil all around. The cops scurried back and forth. The airport workers tried to calm down the passengers, but they failed because there was no any encouraging information. As always, they were talking nonsense, while showing an excessively respectful attitude and apologize. The plane for special government transportation exploded two kilometers away from the runway. Only the flight crew was on board. They all died.

The crash site greeted us with a cool breeze, which, against the background of the dreadful picture, looked like the breath of death. The cars' headlights were illuminating the place of the incident. It's almost 2:30 am. When we arrived, the firefighters have already extinguished the fires that had arisen during the explosion of the plane. Acrid smoke poured from the smoldering objects. The sight is not for the faint of heart. It rained here recently. Everything mixed up in a heap: dirt, wreckage of the aircraft and its internal contents, burned or melted things. Before our eyes appeared the deplorable sight of the mutilated or torn bodies of the flight crew. Involuntarily, goose bumps ran through my skin.

It was difficult to say how far the plane wreckage and his contents were scattered. The specialists will determine it after carrying out an appropriate investigation. For this we must wait for dawn. Holmes's assumptions about the remains of the jewelry after the explosion turned out to be correct. The excitement of replenishment of the country's budget and improvement of the liquidity of the Ukrainian currency disappeared by itself. Various objects were scattered on the ground, but there was not any hint of jewelry.

I could not understand one thing: why would Holmes want to see CCTV recordings? The plane's explosion occurred outside of their range of operations.

- Listen. Why do you need CCTV recordings? What do you want to find there?
- Mycroft said the co-pilot had acute arterial hypotension. The ambulance transferred him to the central city hospital. He felt unwell after taking off Boryspil. The flight attendant measured his blood pressure. It was high. After landing in Odessa, he went to buy the medicine.
- Aren't they examined before departure? How could they allow to him to fly with such health condition?
- According to Mycroft's words, he was absolutely healthy person. There is no medical record that he has any heart disease.
- This means only one thing: he took a large dose of medication, and, because of this, the pressure plummeted. Probably, instead of a first-

aid post, he went to the pharmacy and bought what they advised to him there.

■ Not necessary. He could have been poisoned.

■ Yes. — I sighed. — I think like a doctor. You're like a detective. Who needs to poison him? No, not like this. Who knew that he was in Odessa? How long before departure did they know about the flight? Maybe he was poisoned in Kiev?

■ This is what we need to find out. Upon returning on board, the co-pilot seemed to feel better. Approximately in half an hour his health deteriorated. The first pilot called to the airport medical team. They diagnosed the co-pilot with acute arterial hypotension and sent him to the hospital.

■ What's your point?

■ I think he's a traitor who has fallen into a trap. I give you 99 percent out of 100 that he will die in the hospital. If he is not dead yet. Mycroft sent his men to the hospital to test my guessing.

■ Optimistic way of thinking. There is nothing to say.

■ What to do. This is the reality.

■ Didn't you consider someone shot down the plane?

■ Mycroft is testing this version. But I hardly believe in it.

Ruslan left his people inspecting the plane's damage and returned with us to the airport's building. We went straight to the control room. An airport employee gave Holmes access to CCTV cameras. It was easy to find the second pilot, because we knew where he went. Holmes wrote on the paper the time when he was inside the pharmacy. After buying the medicine, he went to the hall. There he met some man. Looking at his clothes, the man was an airport employee. They went together to the bar.

■ Unbelievable. — I said. — Why did he go to the bar?

■ To meet his death.

Holmes's answer impressed not only me. Ruslan looked puzzled too. Holmes said it so confidently that no one dared to object. We were watching the recording and could clearly see the face of the man with whom the co-pilot had a meeting. Holmes made a photo of this man and sent the picture to his email. He switched on his police program and downloaded the man's photo there. While the program was defining the man's identity, we were observing their conversation inside the bar. Seemed nothing strange was going on there. The unknown man went to the bar and made an order. He returned to the co-pilot with one empty glass and one glass of wine. He put the empty glass in front of the co-pilot. Then he took some box out of the pocket of his work clothes and put it inside co-pilot's bag with medicine. After it, he sat at the table. The co-pilot poured the medicine from the bottle to the glass.

- ■ It looks like a bottle of alcohol tincture of hawthorn. — I said. — Why did he buy the wrong medicine? It's for people who have a low blood pressure. At least he should have bought bisoprolol. For what did he drink the entire bottle?
- ■ See? — Holmes said. — He had high blood pressure and drink the medicine to make the blood pressure higher. Then tell me, how is it possible he got to the hospital with acute arterial hypotension?
- ■ I don't know. It's impossible.
- ■ Indeed. I am more concern what's the box the man put into co-pilot's bag. It's not big enough to make such an explosion.

While we were speaking, the co-pilot stood up and went to the bar. He returned with the bottle of water. Meanwhile, the unknown man poured some powder into pilot's glass and stirred it.

- ■ Bingo! — Holmes said with excitement. — That's how the traitor met his death.

After returning, the co-pilot poured the water into his glass and drank the contents in one gulp. They were sitting till midnight in the bar, and then each went his own way. The co-pilot returned to the plane. The unidentified man went to the room for the airport employees. While we were observing unknown man's action, Holmes looked at the screen of his laptop. His announced shocked us.

■ It's not good. The second man raised from the dead.

He turned towards us his laptop. Our unknown man was looking at us from the monitor. A slight shiver ran through my body. I remembered Kravets and his ability in shooting from a sniper rifle. A thought flashed through my head: "This was the only thing we needed for a complete happiness". I looked at Ruslan. His face became pale with an unhealthy greenish tint.

■ Who is this? — I asked.
■ Zhulikov Ivan. He was the leader of the Zhytomyr's gang who died in a car accident five years ago. — Ruslan answered instead of Holmes. It was obvious he had a history with this man. He continued. — When he was transported from the pre-trial detention center to the prison, KAMAZ rammed the patrol car. The story is simple to the point of banality. The driver fell asleep while driving and died in the hospital. Zhulikov died on the way to the hospital. His corpse, instead of hospital, was taken to the morgue. When we arrived to the morgue, we didn't find the body. After finishing the autopsy, it was immediately cremated. The medical examiners referred to their boss's order.
■ I remember him. My agent fought with Zhulikov, but could not defeat him. His knowledge in Kung-Fu is great. Oh. My second program completed searching. Ha! Another surprise. He is the man from our previous case. Zhulikov killed the Minister of Fuel and Energy. Kravets and Zhulikov is dangerous combination. — Holmes showed to us the second window in his laptop.

It was the program which defines people. Yes. During investigation of the minister's death's case, we faced unknown driver. He masked his appearance, and it was impossible to identify who he was. Now we saw this man. Holmes continued:

■ Ruslan. Go to the airport authorities and find all information which they have about this man. I am sure he changed his name as his appearance. Take his photo with you. Check his telephone and address.

Ruslan left. Holmes was about to say something else, but the ring of his phone interrupted his speech. It was Mycroft. Holmes didn't give Mycroft to say any words. He spoke first:

■ They found the poison in co-pilot's blood..... What next? ... Good. — He hung up. — The co-pilot is dead. The medical examiners found belladonna in his blood. We have nothing to do here.
■ What do you mean? How is about Zhulikov Ivan?
■ Mycroft sent the other team to investigate the aircraft explosion and the co-pilot's death. They'll land soon. We handle this case till their arrival. When they flew here, we'll give them what we found, and our mission will end. We have to fulfill our major task. Let's finish watching the CCTV recordings. I wonder what will Zhulikov do next? Somehow he has to relate to the aircraft explosion.

It was 1:30 am when Zhulikov came out of the room for the airport employees and went towards the runway. Now he was carrying a bag. He left the airport's building and after walking along the wall; he hid behind the pillar a little farther from the special government plane. Soon the helicopter has landed next to the plane. The people from the helicopter carried Tyrin's jewelry onto the plane. After loading, the plane took off. His flight was not long. In a short time, we saw an explosion in the distance. Because Zhulikov was hiding behind the building's pillar, surveillance cameras did not record his action. When he left his hideout, he was closing his bag.

- Zhulikov has exploded the plane. — Holmes stated. — According to my assumptions, he had an apparatus in his bag with which he controlled an explosive device on board the plane. The box, which he gave to the co-pilot, contained an explosive device.
- Can we prove it?
- No. This can be proven by taking him red-handed or if CCTV cameras recorded his actions. We have to find him, but he had plenty of time to escape.
- What about the black box?
- First, we need to find it. I doubt it will give us anything interesting. Perhaps we'll hear a click that notifies about the activation of an explosive device. And what? It will only confirm the rightness of my assumptions. It's impossible to prove Zhulikov's guilt without material evidence.

At this time, Ruslan returned to the control room.

- Zhulikov got a job at the airport almost a month ago under a changed name — Igor Krupin. I called to him on the telephone number which he mentioned in his personal file. The telephone is out of reach. I sent my people to check his address, but unlikely they will find him there.
- We have to contact with the police and announce him in wanted list.
- I already have done it.
- Zhulikov blew up the plane. Look.

Holmes rewound the recording. While Ruslan was watching it, Holmes called Mycroft and told him about the progress of the investigation. After watching the recording, Ruslan asked:

- What about the traitor? Did Mycroft find him?

- Yes. This is one of the jewelry appraisers. He sent two messages to the American number, which we know well. Both messages comprise one word: 1 — "Confirm"; 2 — "Helicopter".
- Was he arrested?
- There is no longer anyone to arrest. Mycroft's men found him dead in his car on the road which lead from Odessa toward Illichivsk. He kept a revolver in his arm. The shot was fired at the temple. Looks like suicide. Only his fingerprints are on the revolver and inside the car.
- Maybe the criminals intimidated him and forced to do it. After he has done dirty deal, his conscience tortured him, and he shot himself. — I said. — He worked for the government, after all.
- Everything is possible, but not in our case. According to the results of the medical examination, he died yesterday afternoon.
- Mystery. — His answer surprise me. — Did someone change the appearance to look like him and came for examination Tyrin's treasure?
- Not necessary. It could be anyone, because the second appraiser has never met him before. It was their first joined work. Thank God there are the cameras in the Tyrin's yard. The police have this man's photo and now they are looking for him.
- Are we going to investigate this case too?
- No, Ruslan. Another group of your department is already in charge of this business. In addition, a plane with other Mycroft's representatives will land soon. He ordered to give them the information about our investigations of the aircraft explosion and Zhulikov. We haven't finished our major task.
- We have nothing to investigate. With the death of Tyrin and Lydia, all ends connecting with the criminal were cut off. Tyutkin cannot speak.
- Murzyan's wife agreed to meet. Yesterday afternoon I called her, but she did not believe in Tyrin's death and rejected my asking. When the news on television confirmed my words, she called me back and invited to the meeting.

- But it's too early to go to her.
- First, we need to have a rest. Who knows what the coming day has prepared for us.

It was almost dawn. Soon we got a call from Ruslan's colleagues. According to their research, Zhulikov did not live at the mentioned address, and no one heard of him. At last Mycroft's group flew in. We gave them complete information about the result of our investigations and set off.

Chapter X: Big fish swallowed the small one

Almost at 6 am we returned to the Holmes's friend's rest house and immediately went to bed. After 3 hours of sleep, we had breakfast and set off to the meeting with Murzyan's wife. Everything looked somehow weird in our investigation. It was about 9 pm when the detective arrived. Already in the evening news, they announced the murder of Tyrin. And in the morning the TV anchormen announced about the death of Lydia Tyutkin. Thank God they did not say under what circumstances she died. The host stated the fact of her death in Tyrin's house and that the investigation was ongoing. But it was already enough to interfere with our work. I guess the news delighted an unknown person from America.

At the exit from the Odessa city, Holmes turned off the road and drove deeper into the outskirts. Murzyan's wife, Elena, was a woman about forty, short, fair-haired with a slight excess of weight. She had two children. Son studied at a construction institute, and the daughter entered this year at a medical school.

- Sorry, Mr. Holmes. I didn't believe you about Tyrin's death. But the evening news confirmed your words. This changed my decision. The major killer is dead. Now I can live in peace.
- Why do you call Tyrin a murderer? Did he threaten your husband?

- He killed him.
- According to the report on the investigation of the incident in prison, your husband was killed by accident. He was walking by the convicts who were fighting. One of them threw a knife at another prisoner. But instead of the convict, the knife hit your husband. This was recorded on camera.
- Have you seen the video?
- No. I read the report.
- This all happened after my husband realized that Tyrin had betrayed him.
- Please tell us more in detail from the very beginning. How your husband met Tyrin? What did they do? Tell all what you know.
- My husband served in the navy. Prior to that, he graduated from the Marinesko Naval College. Upon completion, they awarded him the qualification: junior specialist - navigator. He easily controlled any ship, not to mention small boats. After the army, he went to work on a ship. Ten years ago, Tyrin lured my husband to work under him. He had his own small ship.

  The husband did not like to speak about his job. He always had a good salary. But when we started to get a lot of money, and sometimes old amphora's and coins, it alerted me. On my consistent questions, he retreated and told me the entire story. All the jewelry was imported illegally. When Tyrin was ambassador to Spain, he imported jewelry into Ukraine without a gap. Custom office could not check his belongings. According to Ukrainian legislation, it was forbidden to examine an ambassador's bags.

  When he became the ambassador to Cyprus, things went even more fun. He did not have to come up with a reason to come home. Tyrin negotiated with the captains of the vessels which from Turkey went to Ukraine. He paid them good money for smuggling. Before entering the port of Illichivsk or Odessa, my husband met the ships. He managed

Tyrin's ship. Two people accompanied him. They were devoted to Tyrin to the marrow of bones. If the husband stole something, they would have shot him on the spot. But the parents raised Alexius as a decent person. Before working for Tyrin, he did not take part in any illegal deal. Four years ago, my fears came true. There was nothing suspicious from the start. When he was returning with jewelry, almost near the Tyrin's pier, a sea patrol detained him for inspection. They found the jewelry and arrested my husband, two scuba divers and Tyrin red-handed.

The police released Tyrin in a short time. He visited me and asked about Alexius. What could I tell him? I didn't know where he was. From this time, I looked for him too, but all in vain. About in a month, Tyrin told me that my husband is in the prison. According to his explanation, someone informed the government about their group. He told, when they were arrested, they agreed to tell a fictional story which could not lead to such result. Tyrin didn't know what's going on, and how could it had happened. Because my husband refused to meet Tyrin, he came to me and asked to arrange the meeting. I went to prison immediately, but Alexius didn't want to see me too.

Only in half a year, my husband agreed to meet me. His appearance shocked me. His face's color was gray. The black circles around eyes and shaking hands told me he was ill. I asked for a meeting with the chief of the prison and spoke with him about my husband's health condition. He answered Alexius got flue, and he was in the prison hospital. I should not worry. But after this meeting, husband again didn't want to meet me.

It lasted almost three and a half months. Then a man visited me. He introduced himself as a confidant of Brazilian wanderer. According to him, Tyrin betrayed Alexius and four scuba divers. And If my husband wants to get out of prison, he needs to appeal. He showed to me a flash drive. The flash drive contained the recorded conversation between

78

Alexius and Tyrin, when he asked my husband to take the blame on himself. It was Tyrin's pure admission of crime. The staying the scuba divers in the Mariupol psychiatric hospital confirmed his words. I grabbed onto this advice as a drowning man grabs a straw to stay alive. But in exchange, Brazilian wanderer demanded to describe the location of the sunken Atlantis. If Alexius says yes, he promised to hire an excellent lawyer, and within one year the husband will be free. I agreed to meet Alexius and speak with him about this matter, but with one condition: he will tell about the location of Atlantis after his release from the prison. The confidant of Brazilian wanderer agreed without additional thinking. They probably expected such an answer, or perhaps realized that the second time my husband would not step on the same rake.

In short, it became more fun. My husband didn't want to see me. I went straight to Tyrin and threatened him to tell the truth about their agreement. According to my demand, he had to persuade the chief of the prison to arrange the meeting with Alexius. To my surprise, he did what I told to him to do. Soon my husband agreed to meet me. I retold him my conversation with the confidant of Brazilian wanderer. Alexius allowed to me speak from his behalf. Then I called to the confidant of Brazilian wanderer and confirmed our agreement. He sent the lawyer. Suddenly, on the next day after sending the appeal to the court, I got the call from the prison. They announced to me that Alexius is dead. I am sure it was Tyrin, who bribed the prison staff to organize the Alexius's murder that it should look like as an accidental death. And so it happened. He didn't want someone to find out the location of Atlantis.

- Did you listen to the conversation from the flash drive?
- Why should I? Do you think he could lie to me?
- Everything could happen.
- Do you come to protect Tyrin?

- In no case. I want to know the truth. Do you have evidence about the bribery?
- Not. But this is obvious. It happened on the next day as they sent appeal to the court.
- It really looks very suspicious, but the proverb works here: you can't sew a word to deed. Suspicious without an evidence can lead you in the wrong direction. According to Tyrin's explanation, they agreed to tell the fictional story to the police. The information of the representative of Brazilian wanderer was different. He said Tyrin persuaded Alexius to take the blame on himself. It's look strange. Where is the truth? Why did you believe in his words, but not to Tyrin?
- He showed to me the flash drive. What did I need else? It was my last hope. Tyrin had nothing to offer to me.
- You didn't listen to what was there, but have believed in it. Hmm. Okay.
- Are you judging me?
- This is the privilege of God. I am just analyzing what I heard. In any case, what's done is done. What about scuba divers? Didn't you find out why they were still in the mental hospital? Did Brazilian wanderer want to release them too?
- They were useless for him. According to my husband, when they found Atlantis, only he and the Cypriot guy knew where it was. To avoid the disclosure of sensational secret, Tyrin ordered to blindfold the scuba divers. Tyrin had a navigation log from the bathyscaphe by which he could reach the right place.
- Who is Brazilian wanderer? How did his representative explain to you about their knowledge of the entire story? He had the flash drive with recorded conversation. This conversation had happened inside the prison. How could he get this flash drive? For this aim, he had to have the connection with the chief of the prison. Didn't his arrival alert you?

- According to his words, Brazilian wanderer was a regular buyer of artifacts from Atlantis. Alexius confirmed this. Since they found Atlantis, only one person has bought all artifacts. In most cases, these were not auctions. To avoid price increases and the appearance of competitors, the sale went directly through the auction organizer.
- Unconvincing. At the black auction, people don't know each other. How could he know so thoroughly about your husband's affairs?
- I do not know. The major thing for me was to release Alexius from prison.
- Have you still got the contacts of the lawyer or the confidant of Brazilian wanderer?
- Not. The lawyer came to draw up an appeal, but he did not leave his contacts. I tried to call to the confidant, but his telephone was offline.
- Was there an appeal at all? Maybe it was all a hoax?
- No. The lawyer has done everything as he promised. He brought to me the invitation to the trial.
- Has your husband ever told what happened to the Cypriot man?
- Yes. He told me. When this man was going home, the thieves attacked him. He had jewelry from Atlantis. They killed him and took the jewelry.
- How did your husband know this story?
- That day after their returning from the sea, the Cypriot man did not go home. He wanted to have a drink. Because he didn't come home long time, my husband with the scuba divers went to looking for him. They found him dead on the seashore without jewelry. There were a lot of bruises on his body.

I thought we'll solve some questions when we'll visit the Murzyan's wife. But in contrast, our investigation became more complicated. The received additional information was interesting. Some moments of this story looked weird, and we have to sort it out. Surely it's hard to say anything without the video from the prison. And what's happened to the

Cypriot man in the reality? Elena's story about him and the result of Holmes's investigation were differing. Where is the truth? Since Murzyan's wife told to us everything she knows, we had no choice but to thank her and leave.

Chapter XI: Looking for disappeared evidence

H olmes announced to Ruslan about his intention to go to the police station and to find the video from the prison. Ruslan obeyed. He was with us and listened to the entire Murzyan's story. In a short time, we arrived to our destination. Despite of being surprised, the chief of police ordered to his subordinate to give to us the criminal's case, and allowed to work with it in the meeting room. The first thing which got into our eyes was the name of the detective, who did the investigation. It was Bogdan Semchenko.

■ Do you think it's a coincidence that in both cases the same detective is investigating? — I asked Holmes.
■ It worries me too. If he was a precinct, then it would be easy to check where his plot. If this is not his zone of duty, then we could ask him a question of what he was doing there. The detective can be anywhere. The flash drive with the video not attached to the material of the criminal case. — Holmes called to the policeman who helps to us. He took the call. — According to the description, there is the flash drive with a video from the prison among the case' material. It's missing. Where's it? ...... Oh, good. - Holmes hung up. — We must go to the court. The policeman explained, during the court session, the flash drive was presented as evidence and was withdrawn from the case. But something tells me it's not there.

- Then why are we going to court? Just to waste our time?
- We need to get to the end. Only then we can draw conclusions. Ruslan. Check on your channels who this detective is, Bogdan Semchenko. Are there any sins behind him or he is clean?

In the court, they refused to give to us the case for reviewing without a pre-filled application and getting permission from the chief judge. Holmes had no choice but to call Mycroft and to take advantage of his help. After half an hour, they provided us with the documents of the Murzyan's case. Like documents from the police, Holmes photographed everything without exception. But the flash drive was not in the case. Holmes called the person who brought the documents and asked this question. To which he received the answer: "The signature of the archivist shows that he received a full package of documents with material evidence. It means the flash drive was there. Where the flash drive is now, he does not have the slightest idea. After transferring the file to the archive, he is not responsible for the documents." The circle is closed. We didn't get the desired clarification in the case. But the disappearance of the flash drive confirms Elena's suspicions. The Alexius's death was not the accidental. What was on the video? How can we find it? Suddenly Ruslan's phone rang. He took the call and listened to the respondent. After the conversation he turned to us:

- According to my man, Bogdan is the best detective in the entire city. His father died during fulfilling his duty. He also was the police detective.
- All this is strange and does not fit into the entire picture. - Holmes said and called to someone. The man picked up the phone. — We must meet. I have some questions for you. ...... It will be better this way. We are waiting for you.
- Who are we waiting for?
- Bogdan. He's coming up soon.

After half an hour, Bogdan arrived. We were expecting him in the cars. He offered to go to a cafe which was nearby. Ruslan left his people in the car and entered the cafe with us.

■ I'm interested in the case you investigated almost three years ago. - Holmes began the conversation. - The murder of Murzyan Alexius in prison. Where...

■ I did not investigate this case. - Bogdan interrupted Holmes.

■ In terms of? You signed the report.

■ Right. My signature is on the report, but it was not me who investigated. Pupkin Denis was responsible for this case. The chief of the police called to me, ordered to sign this report and urgently to transfer it to the court. Pupkin's close relative from Russia died. In that day at 4am, Pupkin flew to Moscow, where he changed the other plane. His destination was Tyumen.

■ Did not you have a question with the flash drive? The report says that the judge seized the flash drive as an evidence. As far as I know, when a piece of evidence is seized, you need to make a copy.

■ When I transferred the case to the court, I didn't know if Denis did the copy or not. There was no point in calling and asking, since he was on the plane and would hardly have picked up the phone. I reported to the chief. He said when Denis returns, he will go to court and ask for the copy. After Pupkin's returning, I reminded him about the flash drive. He prepared a special request letter for making the copy. He did it. I saw this request on his desk already signed by the police chief. Later I asked him if the court allowed to him make a copy. He replied that everything was fine. They gave him the copy, and he attached it to the case. What is the actual question? You want to say that a flash drive with the copy of the video is not in the case's materials?

■ Exactly.

■ It's strange. You can ask Pupkin. He is a little distracted. Maybe instead of taking the flash drive to the archive and attached it to the criminal case, he put it in his desk drawer and forgot? Especially he is lost when he needs to check a lot of information. In such cases, Denis will always lose sight of something. The chief knows this Pupkin's feature. Therefore, he is not given hard tasks.

- If the chief does not fire him from the work, it can mean only one thing: someone powerful is behind him. Typically, the detectives investigate the complicated cases. How old is he?

- He is forty. There was a rumor that he had a relative in the Ministry of Defense of Ukraine. But we have no confirmation for it. If he would have had such a roof, then he would have a higher salary. He has a regular salary, like all detectives in our police station.

- This seems even more suspicious to me. Describe him, please.

- Denis is of average height, about a meter seventy. His gait is strange. He walks as if swaying a little. According to his explanation, it was because of a spinal injury. When the doctor was doing to him the manual therapy, he pinched the nerve.

- He does not have one phalanx on the little finger of his left hand.

- How did you find out? Do you know him?

- And he is an excellent fighter. He is very fluent in drunk kung-Fu.

- No. What do you. Pupkin absolutely does not know how to fight. I was told that once on his duty he had to deal with drunk youngsters. They had a fight with guys from another district of Odessa. Denis could not calm down them. Thank God he was smart enough to call for help the second patrol.

- One more question: how did you find yourself at the scene of Tyrin's murder?

- I was supposed to be at home that day. The chief called to me at 7am and ordered to go to the work instead of Pupkin. Because he has eaten something not fresh in the evening, he has terrible diarrhea. When we got the call that someone shot a man in broad daylight, I with my partner left for the scene.

- We have not met your partner. Where was he?
- He was interviewing people who were in the yard.
- And what did he find?
- Nothing. All people were busy with their affairs as a shot suddenly rang out. They didn't understand where sound of shooting came from, and what was going on. Some panicked.
- Was there any car, which was turned the face towards the house from where criminal shot?
- No. There were no cars in the yard. This is the very first thing I checked. Sometimes the information from the DVR is very helpful to the investigation.
- Give me his telephone number. I need to meet Pupkin. But first, I need to check something in the court. Please, don't call him about our visit. Ruslan. Stay here with the detective. Watson. Come with me. Hope we will be back soon.

We left the café. Our return surprised the archivist. But he already treated us more favorably.

- I talked to the detective who signed the report. — Holmes said. — We found out that Pupkin Denis came to you with the letter of request for a copy of the information from the flash drive. When you provide copies, do you register this somewhere?
- Sure. We keep records of who hands things over or takes them, and who makes copies. We need to find the register of that year. Wait. — The archivist went to the closet and searched for the document we needed. Soon he found it and returned to us. — Let's see. When it was?
- June 2007
- The archivist searched for the record. — Here it is. Pupkin came on June 20 and signed for receiving the flash drive.
- Don't you make copies here?

- If I gave him the flash drive, then it was spelled out in the letter. I'll see it now. - He got up and went back to the closet. There he picked up a thick folder and returned to us. — It's the request. Look. Here is the order of the chief judge to issue a flash drive with a return in a week.
- But they did not return it. Do you control such moments?
- Usually yes, but after one day I went on vacation. I left a note to the colleague who replaced me. I wrote he had to monitor the returning of the flash drive. But apparently he did not do it.
- May I speak with your co-worker?
- He retired a year ago. I can give his address.
- Good. Write it and, if it's possible, his phone number.

We thanked the archivist for the information and left. Holmes called to someone. The respondent took the call.

- It's me. I sent you a phone number. Browse the phone book for suspicious numbers and recover all deleted messages. ...... Good. But first find where he is now. I need to meet this person. ...... Yes. I'm waiting. Reset it to me with the program to my phone.
- Do you know who Pupkin is?
- Maybe. One thing is obvious: someone wants to cover up Pupkin and put the blame on Semchenko.

Soon we came to the cafe. Ruslan and Bogdan were sitting at the table and drank juice. Holmes's phone made a sound which announced about the receiving the message. After reading it, Holmes smiled and said:

- We can go to the meeting.

Chapter XII: Criminal with nickname Drunk

Quiet

When Bogdan asked to explain where we were going, he answered evasively. But knowing Holmes, everyone obeyed his decision. Holmes rode with Bogdan. We followed them. We drove along the road towards the city center. In about ten minutes, we stopped. There was a café "White Swan" a little far. Ruslan's car passed us by and stopped from the other side of the café. We continued sitting in the cars. Before setting off to this place, Holmes made an instruction. According to it, we have to stay in the car till he gets off. In a short time, I saw a man came out from the café. He had no time to reach to his car as Bogdan got off and called him. Only they began to walk towards each other, as one man from Ruslan's team got off their van and was walking towards us. It was about fifteen meters between the man and Bogdan when Holmes got off the car. Another two of Ruslan's men got off the van and walked toward us. The man reacted very sharply on Holmes's appearance. He stood still for a moment, then he turned on one hundred eighty degrees and ran. It had happened quickly and looked like a movie clip in slow motion. He almost reached to his car as a Ruslan's employee did him a bandwagon. The man fell down. He did not even have time to react when the other two Ruslan's employees ran up to him and put handcuffs on his hands. Understanding nothing of what happened, Bogdan stood with his eyes wide open. He was in a daze. Walking past Bogdan, Holmes said something to him. This news made his eyes widen even more in surprise. Steve and I were at a distance of them and could not hear the conversation. When we approached Bogdan, Holmes reached the Ruslan's van. They placed the arrested man in his van. Holmes talked to Ruslan about something and returned to us.

- What's happening? — I asked.
- We have caught a very important criminal. His nickname is Drunk Quiet. We'll talk later. Now let's ride behind Ruslan's car. We need to interrogate Pupkin.

We obeyed his order. Holmes got into Bogdan's car again. Steve and I drove behind them. I assumed Ruslan would go to his base, since we were in his city. But I was wrong. We arrived almost on the outskirts of Odessa where there were desolate abandoned several houses. His act is logical. They are a special group. How could he reveal his whereabouts?

While we were on the road, Holmes received information from Pupkin's phone. We entered one house. The roof of the house has been preserved, although in some places there were some cracks. Ruslan brought us to a large room. There was a rectangular table and six chairs around it. Pupkin was seated at the table. Holmes and Ruslan sat in front of him. On one side sat Ruslan's employee. He had a computer for recording the interrogation. The other Ruslan's employees guarded Pupkin from behind. Steve, Bogdan and I were standing behind Holmes and Ruslan. We could see Pupkin's face. He did not express particular concern. Pupkin looked like an ordinary man of about forty, with blond, unkempt hair. His hands were more like a loader's hands. Looking at his dirty nails, it's hard to imagine that a police detective is sitting in front of us. Holmes asked:

- We are looking for the flash drive, which content video from the prison about Murzyan's death. Where is it?
- I returned it to the court.
- There is no entry in the journal about this. I phoned the archivist. He said you didn't return the flash drive. He has sent a letter to the police station demanding the return of the evidence.
- I threw it away.
- Who is behind you?
- No one. I work for myself.
- Don't lie. Who paid you to falsify the investigation of Murzyan's death and to destroy the flash drive?
- He owed me a hundred dollars. I set him up out of hatred.
- Don't you want to talk? Okay. Then I'll tell you this story. You can correct me, if I will not be accurate in details. Ten years ago, you infiltrated a police station to get the necessary information and to cover up the dirty affairs of gangster groups. In early June 2007, you didn't fly to Tyumen for the funeral. You are from Western Ukraine, from Sambir, and you have no relatives in Russia. Your relatives live in Poland. You are a member of the organization "Cleaners". Then in June, you received a task from them to kill the Russian businessman.
- What are you talking about? I went to my friend's funeral and didn't kill anyone. To make sure the chief of police will let me go, I lied about the relative's death.
- All participants of this group have a tattoo on the wrist: there are crossed sword and a broom are entwined with a rose inside an eight-pointed star. Show your wrist.

Pupkin didn't obey, but squirmed in his chair. His eyes ran. One of Ruslan's employees went up to him from behind and picked up both his hands with the wrists up. We saw on his right hand the tattoo which Holmes described.

- Tattoo proves nothing.
- When you fought, Liska Yegor scratched you. With aim to destroy evidence, you have cut his nails. But at this time his brother came to his house. You didn't expect his appearance. Such a mistake. You've forgotten to close the door, and he entered freely. Liska's brother practices kung Fu and has the seventh dan. Even having the knowledge of the drunk kung Fu, you would lose. Knowing this, you hid and waited for a convenient moment to escape. When you were hiding in a closet for long clothes, you dropped one cut off fingernail. The policeman found it during the inspection of the premises. Examination revealed the presence of your DNA. So the denial is pointless. You are wanted in Russia. In Ukraine, you also excelled. Your method of murder is a proof that you were behind it. By beating at important life points, you immobilize your victim. And then you do what your boss ordered to do. Basically, you hang up the victims and all cases are closed with one conclusion: suicide.

It was obvious Pupkin was nervous. But he didn't start talking.

- Who is Brazilian wanderer?

When Pupkin heard this nickname, he looked up. His wide eyes reflected surprise. For a moment he was numb.

- I don't know a person with such a nickname. — He spoke a little stuttering. — Which wanderer?
- Do not pretend to be. I have your correspondence from the phone. Yes, you have deleted them. But I have the program which allows to recover deleted messages in the phone.
- It cannot be the truth. You are bluffing.
- Have you ever thought, if there is a program which allows you to recover deleted files in your computer, then obviously should be the

same program for recovering deleted messages in phones? Now you know it.

At this moment Holmes's phone announced about receiving the message. Holmes picked up his phone and read the letter. Then he turned to Ruslan and said:

■ We need to talk. Watson. Come with me.

We went outside.

■ I got an information about Pupkin's correspondents. One of them looks like his boss. Look. Holmes showed to us the message that Pupkin received from someone on 10th August:

"You have to meet my acquaintance and help to find accommodation. The arrival is on 12th this month. Brazilian wanderer."

■ I presume the message was about Kravets's arrival.
■ You want to tell this is Brazilian wanderer, who sent it? — I asked.
■ No. This message was re-sent. That's why we can see the sender's name. Brazilian wanderer has the direct correspondence with Pupkin's boss. If we find who he is, we'll find Brazilian wanderer. I asked my man to check this telephone number. He faced the problem. Mainly the phone is off line and now as well. Pupkin will be silent. He is afraid for his life. To move our investigation off the ground, we need to find the phone and turn it on.
■ It sounds good, but how can we do it? — Ruslan asked.
■ I received the report about where the owner of the phone has switched it on. This person is in the police station.
■ Just knowing that the phone is in the police station, does not allow to us to determine who it is. The phone must be turned on.
■ And how long will we wait for this moment? We must act now.
■ You say confidently. I guess you have a plan.

- Indeed. Let's go to the police station. I'll connect to the surveillance cameras. We know the date and time when this person sent the message. It gives to us an opportunity look at who was at the police station.
- Message received at 3 p.m. There is always full of people.
- And yet I think it's better than sitting back and waiting for manna from the sky to fall on your head.

Chapter XIII: Who is Brazilian wanderer?

Ruslan had nothing to say to Holmes, and he gave up. Some of his people and the detective Semchenko Bogdan, remained in the abandoned house to guard Pupkin. We set off to implement Holmes's plan. After arrival to our destination, we stopped at some distance from there. It was not in our interests to attract too much attention. In a short time, Holmes connected to the cameras. Ruslan left his people in the van and moved into our car. At 3pm there really were many people at the police station. One group detained the robbers and brought them for interrogation. We deleted the representatives of this group from the list of suspects. There was a meeting in the other department. Usually people go to the meeting without phones. It is forbidden. So we needed not to check this department. It's good that they installed CCTV cameras in this police station in each room and along the corridors. There were no cameras in the chiefs' offices. This simplified our task. Knowing the exact time of correspondence, we looked through each room and each corridor to the question: who was holding a mobile phone. But we found no one. There were five of the management staff in the place and they were in their offices. One of them was Pupkin's immediate superior. We also noticed the head of the personnel department, leaving the toilet at 3:10 pm. At this time, the phone was already disconnected. He held nothing in his hands.

■ Now what? — Ruslan asked. — Do you propose arresting five management staff at once? Or do you think this is Pupkin's boss?

■ I'll find their photos. Then we'll review the recording again. Maybe we missed something. Some of them could go outside or to another office.

Holmes found photos. The fact is, we missed three of them. The chief of the police was in the waiting room and talking with his secretary. Second was in a hidden room and watched the interrogation. The third was at the department meeting. So, two chiefs remained. It's a lot, anyway.

■ Do you offer to arrest these two chiefs?

But Holmes was silent and didn't react at all to Ruslan's question. He continued to scroll through the recordings from the cameras. Soon he found the fourth chief in the corridor. The chief didn't keep the mobile phone in his hands.

■ One left. It's great. Let's go.

■ Do not rush. - Holmes said.

■ Why? You found boss Pupkin.

■ Something does not right here. Did you notice that the head of the organization of cynological activity remained?

■ What is confusing you? Do you think he cannot be a criminal?

■ Any of them can be him. But I'm sure this is the chief of the police. That's why it does not fit to the entire picture of the crime. Think yourself. Pupkin goes wherever he wants. Everyone knows that he is not a skilled detective. There are many young police officers in other departments who would be more useful than Pupkin. But they don't touch him and keep him here. Why? Tell me. Second, on the day, when they planned to kill Tyrin, he had diarrhea. We cannot suspect that a person lied about his illness. It is very punishable by God. But not for the criminal. I consider the option: someone created an alibi for Pupkin that no one would have suspected him in anything. Instead of him, they sent the detective with a pure reputation to the work. Don't you think this is strange? If there were no case with a flash drive, I would suspect nothing either. But this is a double coincidence. Bogdan replaced Pupkin twice. When it had happened the second time, he had the day off. Do you want to tell me in the entire department there were no the other detective on duty who could investigated the Tyrin's murder? There were. But they need the pure detective.

- If we look from your point of view, then your conclusions are logical. But we have no reason to suspect the chief of the police.
- Not yet. I think he works through another link. And this is most likely the head of the personnel department.
- But he was in the toilet.
- The matter of fact, he left the office and went to the toilet at 2:55pm. At 3:10pm he left the toilet. This is exactly the time when the phone was turned on. The question is different: how to arrest the head of the personnel department so as not to frighten away the chief of the police? O. I have an idea. — He called to someone. The respondent took the call. — Mycroft. I need the recording the telephones' conversation the chief of the personnel department of the Central police station in Odessa....... No. Only one day: 10th August till 3:10 pm. No more, no less. — Holmes hung up.
- What's your idea?
- It's elementary. As far as I know the psychology of senior officials, over the years their vanity and megalomania have developed very much. Based on this, I concluded: the chief of the police didn't use the mobile phone when he called to the head of the personnel department. He called to him on the internal phone.
- But he could have called the landline.

- Do you think the conceited person will dial a seven-digit number instead of pressing a single key? Nonsense. In any case, we'll receive wiretapping of both the internal phone and the city.

After some time, Holmes's phone notified of the receiving the message. He opened it and turned on the recording. The first entry concerned a landline telephone. The head of the personnel department answered five calls about employment. We have heard nothing significant. The second file contained his conversations on the internal telephone. There were not so many calls on this phone. Holmes drew our attention to one conversation. It took place at 2:50pm. This is the conversation itself:

"I sent you instructions from the authorities. Monitor the execution of the instructions and report at the end of the execution."

- This may be a normal daily order. And arrest only having this message can entail at best disciplinary action. In the worst case, they will fire me.
- You will not get fired. — Holmes called to someone again. He turned on the speakerphone. It was Mycroft. — There is no time to tell the entire story. I state a fact: according to my conclusions, the chief of the Central police of the city of Odessa has the connection with the boss of criminals with the nickname "Brazilian wanderer". We have no bony evidence which shows his involvement to the crime. To confirm the correctness of my assumptions, we need to arrest the chief of the police and find his phone, which he uses to communicate with the underworld. If I'm wrong, I ask Ruslan and his group not to punish. They were under my command and carried out my orders.
- Good. I give my word. All will happen as you said. May God bless you.
- Holmes hung up. — I have resolved the question. Now on the way.

■ Listen. You amaze me. — Ruslan looked embarrassed and confused. — I heard you are genius and honest, but that's too much. We work together. How can you take full responsibility? You think I ...

■ First, you really were sent under my leadership. - Holmes interrupted Ruslan. - Second, one wise man said: "Who praises the other one, looks like a person who is putting the footboard for the running man." Stop ranting. We are losing precious time. Let's do it.

For fulfilling this task, Ruslan called to his subordinates from the van. Three men came for helping. After listening to Holmes's instruction, we entered the police station building. Ruslan and one of his man went with us to arrest the chief of the police. The other two his men got an order to arrest the chief of the personnel department.

The secretary of the chief of the police announced him about our arrival. Referring being busy, he refused admission. Despite this, we entered his office. The secretary tried to protest; she called the police officer on duty to force us out of the building. But when she saw how Ruslan handcuffed her boss, she was numb with surprise or horror. The attendant who ran to her call, also stopped at the door. Seeing Ruslan's personal sign, he had no choice but to obey. As you can see, he and his group are endowed with such great powers. We placed the chief of the police in the room's corner. He was sitting on a chair. To avoid him trying to poison himself, we handcuffed him in such a way that his hands were behind him. Ruslan's man and Steve were assigned to guard him. Because Holmes did not find the phone in the police's chief clothes, the three of us began to search the room. It was obvious the boss was nervous, although he tried not to show it.

Soon the Ruslan's employees called. According to their report, they quickly completed the task and switched on the phone. Then they transferred the offender to the interrogation room. Ruslan gave them the permission to start the interrogation without him. Holmes called his friend and notified about turning on the phone. Now it remains to wait for the information.

It was more difficult with the chief of the police. We could not find his secret phone. The chief did not answer on our questions. He kept silence. After inspecting the table, Holmes went to inspect the bookcase. It turned out like in a children's game, in which you had to find something. To do this, the children made tips: cold - if they were looking in the wrong direction, warmly if they turned in the right direction or hot - if they were very close to the aim. So it was here. Looking at the expression on the face of the chief of the police, it became clear that Holmes was on the right track. He was calm, but turned pale. The pupils of the eyes widened, probably out of fear. In order not to betray himself, he lowered his eyes and looked at the floor. Ruslan and I joined Holmes. The search went faster. In the second row, Ruslan found a telephone inside the book. Someone cut out the groove there. Then he with his man took the chief of the police to the second interrogation room. Holmes and I stayed in the office. He turned on the phone. As expected, it was empty. Only one number was recorded in the phone book, signed as "Superior". Holmes called his friend and gave a new task. On this, we finished our search in the chief's office and went to the interrogation room.

When we came to the hidden room, we were notified that the chief of the police requested a lawyer. In this, no one dared to refuse him. Now we were waiting for his appearance. The head of the personnel department also demanded the lawyer. Soon we got the result of checking the phone of the head of the personnel department. Holmes was right again. He was the link between the chief of the police and Pupkin. There were no other numbers in the phone book, no calls or correspondence using other subscriber numbers. Then we received information from another phone. There was one respondent there. He or she registered with two numbers. One number was served by Ukrainian telecom operator, the second — an

American one. Both the first and second number were offline. Holmes compared the American number with the number from which someone contacted with Tyrin and Lydia Tyutkin. It was the same number. Analyzing the entire correspondence chain with the help of five phones, we concluded: the supreme boss of this company is a man with nickname — Brazilian wanderer. But who is he or she? It is hard to say. Even if this person switches on the phone, it will give to us nothing. Brazilian wanderer never wrote messages to the chief of the police. He always called to him. Then the chief wrote the message to the head of the personnel department and signed it on behalf of Brazilian wanderer. Everything is so confusing.

As soon as the lawyers arrived, they demanded an audience with their wards. The negotiations lasted for about half an hour. After having consulting with lawyers, both suspects spoke. But we didn't expect what we heard.

The interrogation of the chief of the police:

- Who is Brazilian wanderer?
- It's me.
- Do not lie. You have a secret phone that identifies one respondent. Who is it?
- This is my lover. I am hiding my relationship with another woman from my wife.
- Why did you kill Tyrin?
- I didn't kill anyone. And I don't know who Tyrin is.
- You order to Pupkin to meet someone on August 12 of this year. Who is this?
- He met my mistress.
- Where did she settle?
- In my secret apartment.
- Pupkin is a killer who is wanted both in Russia and in Ukraine.

- Bullshit. He cannot kill an ant. His religion forbids doing this. He is only suitable to clean the toilets. I put up with him because he holds his mouth shut.
- But he can take advantage of your weakness and start blackmailing you.
- He will not do it. Who then will hire him? He is under my full control.
- Why did you choose such a nickname?
- This is the name of one of the most poisonous spiders. And I am the spider that keeps order in the city. Representatives of the underworld should be afraid of me.

The interrogation of the head of personnel department:

- Which the work did you do for the chief of the police?
- Different. The last one was about his lover.
- Why did he use Pupkin for this aim?
- Pupkin is an unexperienced detective. He bribed the chief of the police. After this, he fulfills different tasks, which the chief ordered to him to do.
- Do you know that Pupkin is a killer?
- Come on. He even cannot fight. I saw how he ran from the bandits by my own eyes.

Everything turned out so smoothly for them, as if they agreed. However, the way it was. We asked to them many tricky questions, but received the most stupid answers that did not suit us. They played an excellent performance. It was already 8 pm, but we were still crumbling the water in a mortar. We left the interrogation room for a short meeting. Ruslan's men were also invited for interrogating the second suspect. At the meeting, we unanimously decided to transport the suspects to the pre-trial detention center. It was dangerous to leave them in the police. Already we had terrible experience when we left the criminals in the police. Pupkin will be send to Kiev by plane, where he will be placed in a secret investigative shelter. Since the major players' plaid their game, we cannot accuse him of.

We called a special car to transport the suspects to the detention center. Before her arrival, the lawyers demanded to feed their wards. When Holmes heard this demand, it alerted him. To avoid the incident with the poisoning of suspects, Holmes took appropriate measures. Ruslan suggested using the services of a particular cafe. He didn't mention the name of the cafe inside the police building. Holmes sent Steve to bring the food. Ruslan made an order by phone when he went outside with Steve. That is, when Steve will arrive, the food will be almost ready and he will need to pay and pick it up. The cafe was nearby the police station, because within forty minutes Steve returned. The policeman was present in the interrogation room during the meal. Finally, the transport arrived, and we sent the suspects to a pre-trial detention center. Pupkin was sent from Odessa International Airport to Kiev by special state plane. Thank God we had no problems with sending him. No one, except the detective Semchenko Bogdan, knew about his arrest.

Chapter XIV: No signs of trouble

■ Now what? - Ruslan asked Holmes. - What are your plans?

■ It's necessary to confirm whether Pupkin met the chief's mistress. Ask the airport for cooperation. We need their cameras' recordings for August 12th. I doubt in his confession. According to my assumption, Pupkin met Kravets. You know the city and its surroundings well. Request recordings from all the city cameras that are on the way leading from the airport till the house where Kravets lived. It would be nice for us to eat. We worked without lunch, and already almost 9:40 pm. Second, we need to decide on the overnight stay.

■ We can have dinner in the same cafe where we ordered the food for the suspects. I'll make an order. While we arrive, the table will be set.

■ Good. I will pay for everyone, including your group. So, don't infringe your choice.

■ Thank you. About the night. We have our departmental recreation facility. It's toward Nikolayev when leaving Odessa. We can stay there. There are always free rooms for such an event.

Holmes agreed. Upon our arrival at the cafe, they have already served the table. First, we ate the cold appetizers. Then waitresses brought the hot dishes. The dinner was superb. After dinner, we went to the recreation facility. Holmes offered to Ruslan to send his subordinates home, but he refused. He referred to Mycroft's order to protect our group like the apple of an eye. It flattered me to hear this.

We arrived at our destination somewhere after half an hour. The building was built in Sovdep era. But it was cozy inside. The rooms were well maintained, nothing more. Because the rooms were small, they accommodated us in the event hall. Holmes closed the door from the inside. Ruslan warned the management of the recreation facility so they would not bother us. We came not to rest, but to work. While we were going here, Ruslan received the information from video surveillance cameras. There was a lot of information, but we had four computers at our disposal. This simplified the task. Ruslan's employees, who were not involved in viewing the recordings from the cameras, were resting.

Before viewing the recordings, Holmes showed the Kravets's photo. We had two goals: to find Pupkin and Kravets. Holmes launched the special program. This program determines the location of the person from the photo. It saved a lot of our time and released us from unnecessary viewing all the records. But we found neither one nor the other on the airport cameras' recordings. We found Pupkin with a passenger in the back seat in the recordings from the city cameras. It was difficult to determine who was sitting behind. He was driving from the airport along the path that Ruslan indicated.

■ We cannot distinguish on the recording it's a man or a woman. This is the dead end. — Ruslan said with sadness. — I have to release the chief of the police.

Holmes did not answer on his words. I'm not quite sure whether he heard at all Ruslan, or he completely went into studying the recordings. Ruslan embarrassed and left Holmes alone. But as it turned out, Holmes heard everything. After a while, he spoke. His answer struck all of us.

- God has no dead ends. It's people, in their weakness or lack of faith, came up with such a concept. Where's this place? - He pointed to the building. We saw Alfa Bank there. The name of the street was not visible. The video showed that Pupkin's car stayed third at the crossroads and was waiting for the green light comes on. On the corner of the building, there was a bank. His cameras were turned towards the car.
- I know where it is.
- We are going there.

We set off to the new destination. Ruslan left part of his group at the recreation facility. His car drove ahead of us, showing the way. I realized what Holmes was going to do. But how will Ruslan take it? I think Holmes doesn't care at all. In such situations he always says: "In the name of revealing a big crime, I think Motherland will forgive me a little one". When we arrived at the desired building, Ruslan moved into our car. He calmly reacted to the fact that Holmes broke the password of Alfa Bank cameras and connected to them. Since we knew the exact time when the car was near this building, this simplified our searches. Holmes quickly found the record and turned on the video. The video clearly showed who was sitting on the back seat of the car. It was a man. He had straw-colored hair. His magnificent mustache had the same color. He was wearing glasses. We could not define who he was, but it was enough to refute the chief' lie.

- Because we have to act under the law, — Holmes said to Ruslan, — tomorrow ask this bank for recordings from their cameras. When we return to the recreation facility, I'll try to determine who this man is by the contours of the face.

Upon arrival back, Holmes launched his police program to identify Pupkin's passenger. After a short time, we saw the result of processing the photo: the man's face corresponded to the shape of the Kravets's face on

87 percent. Now the chief of the police has no way for retreating. We revealed his lie. It would be nice if Pupkin speak. With such encouraging thoughts, we went to bed.

It was 6:25 am when we have woken up by alert. The chief of the police hanged himself. Not only that, in the evening news TV anchor announced about his arrest. Now what will happen? Why did he commit suicide? We quickly packed up and set off.

The head of the pre-trial detention center, Yury Biryukov, met us. He was about fifty-five, a gray-haired, stocky man. His short hair was neatly combed. The officer on duty raised him by alarm. He arrived a little earlier than us. By his appearance, we could easily determine that he was very nervous. This is not surprising. We rarely find such emergency situations in life. In my memory, this is the first time. These scenes we can often watch in the films.

- ■ Who is the first discovered Durasov? — Holmes asked.
- ■ One of our guard. It is customary for us to go through the corridors of the isolator at a certain time and inspect each chamber through the window. The inspection began at 6 in the morning. As soon as the attendant saw the hanged man, he immediately called me. I ordered to notify you.

No one touched the things inside the chamber. Durasov hung himself on the sheet, tying it to the window grill. When Holmes and Ruslan examined the body, they allowed to remove it and put on the bed. Except for slight scratches and a bruise on his left hand, there were no visible signs of a struggle.

- ■ Did he sleep with his feet to the door? — Holmes asked the guard, who found the deceased.

- Yes. When I was making the inspection at 11pm, he lay with his head to the window. But he was alive. We exchanged some phrases.
- He was killed.
- It's impossible. — The head of the pre-trial detention center objected Holmes's assumption.
- Show me the cameras' recordings.
- What is the basis of your conclusion that he was killed? — Ruslan asked.
- Scratches and a bruise on his left hand indicate that Durasov was sleeping when someone began to choke him with a pillow. He was beating his hand against the stone. During an autopsy, the medical examiners will find the sleeping pills in his blood.

Ruslan asked no more questions. Holmes gave the reasoned enough answer. We sent the body of the chief of the police to the examination.

On our way to the room, where we were intending to watch the cameras recordings, I said:

- Don't you think you need to order to guard the head of the personnel department more carefully?
- No. Nothing will happen to him. He was an intermediary who knew nothing. You can torture him as much as you like, but it will not give any results. Only the chief of the police was dangerous for the criminals, because he spoke directly with the head of the criminal world.

The computer room was empty, but looked normal. I would say — as in many films. There was a table, chairs and many computers connected to the certain cameras. Holmes sat at the table and began to work with the computers. He found the right recording and switched it on. We saw on the recording nothing strange till midnight. At 12:05am the security guard entered the cell to the chief of the police. In twenty minutes he went out of there. Could the guard kill the chief of the police? Or it was something else. It's forbidden to come inside the chamber. But it was not an ordinary prisoner. We continued to watch the recording, till the guard noticed the corpse. There was no doubt left. The staff member in a pre-trial detention center killed Durasov.

- Who does this employee work with?
- Bunin Ivan works in this room. He monitors the suspects through cameras.
- Where is he?
- He must be here. The change will come at 8am. We must look for him.

There are few places in the detention center where he could hide. We found Bunin in one of the toilet cubicles. The sight was unpleasant. He was sitting on the toilet. There were a lot of vomit masses around him on the floor. Also, a small plastic bottle from the medicine was lying there. The head of the detention center picked up the bottle. According to the inscription, it was the bottle of the digoxin, which contains 50 pills. But it was empty. Digoxin is a cardiological preparation that contains digitalis glycosides. The drug itself is a good, but it must be used very carefully. Digitalis herb has many contraindications. In large doses, digitalis glycosides act as a strong poison. In the best case, an overdose leads to the poisoning of the body. It can cause the death in the worst case. Bunin drank 50 pills and died. His body is not stiff yet. This means he died recently. The guards pulled him out of the toilet cubicle and laid on the floor. During the search of Bunin's clothes, Holmes found a note. Here is its content:

"I ask you to forgive me for what I did. Yesterday, an unknown person kidnapped my ten-year-old daughter. At 9 pm a man called me and threatened. If I want to see my daughter alive, I must kill the chief of the police. Ivan Bunin."

■ So similar. And again he did not leave a single trace.
■ What are you talking about? — Biryukov asked Holmes. — Did you know that Ivan had the connection with criminals?

But Holmes did not answer. He has already left the men's room. Unlike Biryukov, I understood who Holmes was talking about. He mentioned the professor Moriarty. It was his method. Biryukov caught up Holmes in the corridor and demanded the explanation. Holmes gave the short, but convinced answer: "I mentioned the other person, but the information is classified". After checking Bunin's phone, we confirmed his words. Holmes dialed the number from which the offender called Bunin yesterday evening, but there was no answer. The phone was turned off. He called the wife of the deceased. According to her, the criminals have not yet returned child. We sent the police patrol to their home. Upon arrival, they examined Bunin's house and confirmed the child's absence. While they were in the house, the unknown drove up to the yard and dropped off the child. Then they just disappeared. This once again confirmed inadequate competence of our law enforcement agencies. But we were lucky. There was the car on the opposite side of the road. This car's DVR recorder recorded the criminal's car arrival and departure. The policeman called the owner of the car and took the DVR for examination. At the police station, we watched the recording. We saw the driver. He had blond, straw-colored hair and a fluffy mustache of the same color. Surely you understood with whom we faced again. Yes, it was Kravets. And now what? The circle is closed. We have no clue to continue the investigation further.

We went to the morgue. The medical examiners almost finished making the autopsy. Holmes's guessing appeared to be true. They discovered the marks of the sleeping pills in Durasov's blood.

■ You said that God has no dead ends. And what's this? We have entered an even greater impasse and there is no way out.

■ This is not a dead end. The head of the criminal gang, let's call him Brazilian wanderer, shows his fear. He hurries to cover his tracks. Today he succeeded. But what will happen tomorrow? Anger is the wrong word to describe his emotional state. He is furious. When a person is furious, he is more prone to make mistakes. And when he makes the mistake, we'll use it.

■ We can wait for ages till it will happen.

■ No. He does not have so much time and moral strength. If Brazilian wanderer and the professor, with whom I have been fighting since the end of this year's spring, are the same person, then we cut off too many paws of this vile and evil spider. Perhaps this is his last paw, from where he received the big profits. He lost the location of Atlantis. I reflected on why Pupkin covered up Tyrin's crime of killing Alexius, if he works for another criminal. And I came only to one explanation: Tyrin was the last person who knew the exact location of the extraction of ancient artifacts from the sunken Atlantis. I am sure he made a great effort for deciding to kill Tyrin.

■ From the beginning Brazilian wanderer seduced Lydia Tyutkin to kill Tyrin. Now you announced that he didn't want to kill him. Why do you think so?

■ It was nothing more than a manipulation. Four years ago, something happened between Brazilian wanderer and Tyrin. Tyrin had to say goodbye to his post as ambassador. Do you think he left because he was tired of earning millions of dollars and just decided to live on retirement? Nonsense. I don't believe in this. Another option is more suitable for this story. Brazilian wanderer planned to notify Tyrin of the trap. Thanks to the warning, Tyrin remains alive and immensely grateful to Brazilian wanderer. After such a situation, he expected the warming of their attitude, and possibly a resumption of cooperation in the search of artifacts and their sale.

■ But if this is not one person, but two different?

111

■ Then this man is not angry, he is maddened. We deprived him of the only way of enrichment. But, though, something tells me this is the same person. I have not heard about appearance a new group of criminals in Ukraine with a large branching in the spectrum of activities.

Chapter XV: She had to die

Holmes has offered ending the investigation on Tyrin with a trip to Illichivsk. Surely it would be foolish not to examine the bathyscaphe. Though, it was unlikely we'll find something useful there for our investigation. But as Holmes always says: "we need to examine every clue which comes across our path". Today is Saturday. While we were driving from Odessa to Ilyichivsk, Ruslan phoned to the director of the Port and received the permission to inspect the Tyrin's bathyscaphe. When we arrived to the destination, the guards allowed us to enter the port without problems. One guard showed to us the bathyscaphe's location. It was the first time I saw such an object. Its size was impressive: the length — 8 meters; height — about 4 meters; wide — slightly less than 4 meters. The bathyscaphe is equipped with a special manipulator. The contract states that it can lift objects to the surface weighing up to 200 kilograms. Availability of equipment explained how they picked up the statue of Nereid riding a dolphin from the depth of the sea. Inspection of the bathyscaphe gave nothing. Ruslan notified the director of the Illichivsk port about Tyrin's death. Also, he warned that until completing the investigation, the director has to protect the underwater vehicle from theft.

From Ilyichivsk we went to Nikolayev. Steve drove the car. Holmes was sitting next to him and was silent. My curiosity overwhelmed me, and I asked:

- Are we going to inspect Tyutkin's house?
- Yes. But only after visiting the police station. I found the photos on the Internet with the title: "Helplessness of the police and the mafia showdown". The photo shows a battered sedan. It's the same car which the bandits used during Tyutkin's robbery. Someone used the weapon in this attack. There are two holes in the windshield, and there is blood on the seats. Probably the passengers were killed. Three corpses lay near the car. The information about two other persons is missing.
- Do you think one gang attacked the other?
- Not excluded. We'll find out about it in the police.

Less than in three hours we arrived to the police station. Because it was the weekend, we again used Ruslan's authorities. He called to the chief of the police and got the permission to learn the case. The policeman on duty met us and led to the meeting room. Soon he brought the case and left. Holmes opened his laptop and compared the silver-colored sedan from the CCTV recordings, which we got with Gregson's help, and the car from the criminal case that got under the attack. The result was stunning; it was the same car.

- It means someone, so brave or stupid, dared to steal the ancient artifacts from the professor Moriarty. — I said. — Unbelievable.
- It doesn't matter they are brave or stupid. The fact is, they or he will live not long on this Earth.

Then we looked at the photos on which the corpses of the dead were captured. All five people were dead. The case contained the results of the autopsy with photographs. According to the autopsy, someone killed these men using the Kalashnikov assault rifle. Examining the photos, we noticed that all the dead on their wrist had a tattoo in the form of an eight-pointed star, with a crossed sword and broom inside. The place of their intersection was entwined with a rose. This tattoo is a confirmation of their affiliation with the organization "Cleaners". This also confirmed the agreement between Lydia and her American correspondent. It all fits together. One thing is not clear: where does the robbers with the Kalashnikov assault rifles came from? Ukraine is considered as a civilized peaceful state.

- How can gang of criminals have this weapon?
- Dear Watson. Many representatives of the underworld have such weapons. And this is an indisputable fact. I care about something else. What is this gangster group? In my practice I have never met daredevils who dare to go against the cleaners. Did another criminal's group appear in Ukraine, more powerful than cleaners? Ruslan. Did you hear something about this?
- No. For today, the organization of cleaners is the strongest. The representatives of other groups have always obeyed them.
- This is becoming extremely interesting. Although the case has not yet been closed, but the detective already marked it as a dead. There is no evidence or the clue which points who did it. They attacked in the deserted place. The road is in the middle of the field. There is no imprint of other cars. This suggests that the attackers left their car somewhere else. Surely, near to the site of the attack. Strangely, there is no the detectives' report about looking for the attackers' transport in the criminal case. Didn't they wonder how culprits got to such a deserted place? At least, they had to have a car. We can go today and look for car's prints. But I think it'll be in vain. Six days have already passed. Moreover, many policemen, correspondents and curious persons visited the crime scene. We will not distinguish the criminals' car after such many visitors. So pity. I'll photo the case and we'll go to the Tyutkin's mansion.

Since the police of the city of Nikolayev opened the criminal case as regarding the murder of Lydia Tyutkin, they had already examined her house. When we arrived to the mansion, we saw the police car standing near the gate. As soon as we stopped, the policemen got out of the car and headed for us. Ruslan showed his documents and explained the situation. They allowed to us to enter the house. The house was large, three-story with attics. There were the flowers and fruit trees in front of the house. Tyutkin did an expensive repair inside the house, but not using the same exotic decoration as the Tyrin's house. It was an ordinary house of the wealthy family. Furniture matched the style of the residents. I suppose they imported furniture, and it was expensive. We didn't see the antiques in the house. The policeman showed to us the owner's office. The room was large, approximately 20 square meters. There was a safe in the corner. The writing desk is near the window, deployed facing the door. I can't imagine how this didn't annoy Tyutkin. It's hard to work when the sun constantly shines on the monitor. The room is on the east side. Or he worked in the evening. There are the bookcases on both sides of the room. Tyutkin placed the table and eight chairs in the center of the room.

Holmes sat down at Tyutkin's computer. We had to check with whom Lydia corresponded to open a current account in the offshore zone. But her email did not contain such information. There was only a letter from the bank in Cyprus about the opening of a foreign currency account. We were lucky. Lydia left the contract with the bank on the table. There we found the detailed password information for entering the bank system. Holmes opened an online bank and entered a password. In a short time, we saw the interface of an international client bank with account balances. But the balance of the account was zero.

- What's this? — Ruslan asked. — In the correspondence, Lydia confirmed the receipt of money. Did she spend $5 billion?
- I have no idea. — Holmes answered. — Let's check the bank statement for July 26th. — After a few seconds, a bank statement for the specified

date was opened. Holmes read the information. — Lydia received the money from the American company "Mr. Pete and Ukrainian Cuisine". What does the cuisine have to do with it? Did she sign the contract with this company? — Holmes began to rummage through the papers were on the table. He found this document. It was in an envelope under the papers. Holmes read the contract. — This is an agreement for opening a new Ukrainian restaurant in California in San Francisco. Cool. They hired Lydia as an adviser to the general director for organizing the work process and arranging the restaurant business.

- Does someone pay such fabulous money to the consultant?
- Certainly not. It's one of the way for avoiding to mention the actual name of the goods. They cannot sign the contract for the sale of the ancient artifacts. Even offshore banks would not miss such a payment. I thought only in Ukraine the criminals use such a scheme for money laundering. But it turns out I was wrong, or Brazilian wanderer comes from Ukraine.
- But where is the money?
- Let's check it. We just need to open a bank statement for the period from July 26 till today.

While the computer was loading the information he had been given, Holmes returned to reading the agreement between Lydia and the American company. Holmes laughed.

- WOW! I have never seen that scammers came up with such a clause in the contract. Moreover, the bank approved it. Amazingly.
- What are you talking about?
- Look. The contract states the company hired Lydia as the consultant for 1 year. Payment is made in two payments. They have to make the first payment within 10 days from signing the contract. The second payment is August 20th. They signed the agreement on July 20. The bank must accept a scanned copy of the contract for work with the

subsequent provision of the original. The parties agree to provide the original contract to the bank within a month from the first transaction.

At this time, the computer opened the bank statement for the specified period. The bank returned the money to the customer of the services in connection with force majeure - the death of the service provider.

- Lydia died on Thursday, August 19th. Today is August 21st. The bank produced the refund too quickly. What documents confirm force majeure? — Ruslan asked.
- Let's read the contract. — Holmes opened the section of the contract, which spelled out the above circumstances, and read. — "To fulfill the terms of this agreement, the sudden death of the contractor is the force majeure circumstance. This circumstance is confirmed by a scanned copy of the report of the forensic experts. In the event of such the circumstance, the bank must return the money to the customer within two days from receipt of the scan copy. The original report of the forensic experts has to be sent to the bank within a month from the force majeure circumstance". Now everything is clear. Lydia was killed on the 19th in the evening. On August 20, someone. No, not like this. Kravets received the copy of the result of the forensic experts and sent it to his boss. And if we say "his boss", then the professor Moriarty enters the ring. From this we can conclude: Brazilian wanderer and the professor Moriarty are the same person. On Friday, August 20, the bank returned the money to the account of the American company. Dashingly, they covered Lydia. According to this scheme, they definitely didn't leave to her the other choice, only to die.
- It seems like that. — Ruslan said. — But we don't have a single clue which points to the professor Moriarty.
- This is his strong point: "To disappear from the scene of the crime imperceptibly and cover up the tracks so no one could dig against him". It's necessary to contact the detective from Nikolayev who is

investigating this case. What did he find in her office? I would like to see the content of the safe.

Holmes called the detective, and he kindly agreed to drive up to us. Soon he arrived. From his words, he found nothing in her office. It confirmed the Lydia's story, which she told to us in Kiev. She was the deputy director only on the paper. In fact, her father led the entire workflow through the Internet while sitting in his office at home. So there was no point in going to the office. All working documents were in this room. The detective also confirmed having the keys from entire Tyutkin's property. He received it from Odessa's police station. With their help, we opened the safe and examined the contents. There were stored some valuables, checkbooks, bank cards and other documents of a financial and business nature. Tyutkin used the safe for the job, not for home needs. We studied all documents, which were in the house. In the result, we found nothing, what could relate to our case.

Chapter XVI: The authentic story of treasure hunters

After examining Tyutkin's mansion, we went to have dinner. It was about 7pm when we returned to our rented apartment. The last three days have been so busy with work that absolutely everyone rejoiced at the appearance of a free evening to relax. Ruslan came with us. His group went to another apartment, which was next to ours on the same floor. As soon as we crossed the threshold of the apartment, Holmes's phone rang. Everyone stood waiting for the order to go somewhere again. It was Mycroft. Holmes turned on the speakerphone:

■ I'm reporting the good news. Tomorrow you can meet with Tyutkin. He is not quite healthy. In order to recover from the harm caused by drugs, he still has to undergo a full course of treatment for about two weeks. This morning he felt better and was adequate to communicate. Unfortunately, Tyutkin heard on the TV news of his daughter's death. He tried to escape from the hospital to see Lydia. The doctor gave to him the sedative, because his shouting turned into the hysterical lamentation. During his attempt to escape, he was scattering the surrounding objects. He made the total mess in his hospital's room. But the doctor promised that by the morning he will be normal again.

■ Great. Perhaps he will take off the curtain from this story with Atlantis. At least from some part of it.

■ According to the doctor, Tyutkin has no schizophrenia. He was diagnosed incorrectly. Because of the attack on his house and the murder of his wife, he got the psychological trauma. The doctor had to send him to the rehabilitation center, but he didn't. For today, he has the troubled post-traumatic syndrome. Since the diagnosis was incorrect, the doctor prescribed the wrong medications. That's why, instead of improving, the pills caused a deterioration in his state of health as hallucinations, anxiety, panic attacks and aggressiveness.

It reminded me of my friend's words: if you do nothing like that, then you can't even imagine this is existing. I doubted his saying. It looked weird. Today the Tyutkin's story proved the righteous of his words. Looking back and scrolling through my mind before I met Holmes, I feel myself like a child with pink glasses on. I have an ordinary life as many people have: went to school, graduated from the university, found the job, met my love and so on. I have never thought about criminals and their activities, about corruption or something like this. How many people like me live without understanding the reality or don't pay attention on it? After the adventures with Holmes, the veil fell from my eyes. The entire world is mired in crime. Where are we going? This is the wrong way. But for people who are used to living off deceit and crime, this seems like a normal existence. Yes. This is the right word for description of their life — existence, but not the life. Will the world ever return to the normal life? Looking at everything that happens, I think that is unlikely. And if this happens, then probably it will not be soon.

On the next morning, we drove to the hospital. The doctor met us and led to Tyutkin's room.

■ My name is Sherlock Holmes. This is my colleague Dr. Watson, and investigator Ruslan. On Monday 16th August, the bandits attacked you. Your daughter hired me to investigate this case. From her words, on that day you took the valuable ancient artifacts from the bank. When you were driving home, the bandits attacked you and stole the treasures. Can you describe the criminals and tell in detail how it had happened?

■ I told the detective everything and I have nothing to add. Because of the stress, I don't clearly remember how and what happened. My driver can tell more. He is in this hospital too, only in a different department.

■ Please tell us how you met with Tyrin. When did you start trading the ancient artifacts?

■ I don't know what you are talking about. What's the artifacts? I have my restaurant business in Nikolayev and two galleries in Odessa.

■ When your daughter came to me in Kiev, she wore a necklace of coins worth 120 thousand dollars. Coins are ancient. According to my assumption, they were made in Atlantis. Tyrin discovered the location of the sunken civilization five years ago. Since then, these coins have often appeared at the black auctions. Their cost is 3 thousand dollars for one. The length of your daughter's necklace is 80 centimeters. The diameter of one coin is 2 centimeters. I think you have not forgotten how to count?

■ You are confusing something. It's...

■ Anton. — Holmes interrupted Tyutkin. — Stop lying. This is not in your favor. If you tell everything from the start, you'll reduce your prison sentence. The photos from the morgue prove my words. — Holmes took the copy of the results of the Lydia's autopsy from the bag and showed to Anton one photo. — See? This is the necklace I told you about. The experts have confirmed this is not a fake. It's an ancient artifact. In addition, someone killed Tyrin.

■ There he is, dear. — Tyutkin's voice changed. He crossed his arms, tilting the head a little to the right. Anton squinting eyes and looked straight at Holmes. The hard smile appeared at his face. What's this? Is he gone crazy? He continued his speech: — It's God punished him for sending the robbers to my house. He is responsible for my wife's untimely death. I trusted him. — The loudness of his voice increased and with it the danger of a hysterical fit increased. — And how did he repay me for my loyalty? A? Look at me. What a miserable position I am now in. - He began to shake and wringing his hands. A reddening of the face and engorged of the vein on his neck scared me. If it last little longer he will faint. The loud crying about the plight turned to the hysterical. Thank God the doctor was here. He intervened into the conversation.

■ Anton. Calm down, please. Yesterday we agreed, you'll tell to the detectives everything what you know. It will help them find the criminals.

■ These are all the Tyrin's tricks. He sent the bandits to rob me. During the year after his retirement, Tyrin became impoverished. He led the miserable life. It was he who attacked me. — Anton again started screaming. — I wanted to share the jewelry with people to whom we owe our wealthy life.

■ Who are you talking about? — Holmes asked.

■ I wanted to clear myself of this debt. — Seemed Tyutkin didn't hear the question. He was busy with his reasoning and continued to speak with himself. — But how did he find out when I'll take the jewelry from the bank? It means there is a traitor in my house.

■ Stop. — The doctor again intervened in the conversation. — You wind yourself up. If you are tired, we can reschedule the meeting for another day. The detective can ...

■ There can be no other day. — Holmes interrupted the doctor. — Tyrin was not a beggar. He hid his condition. And this means someone influential hunted him.

■ I don't believe you. You are lying. — His eyes narrowed even more and his speech became muffled, like the hiss of a poisonous snake. He leaned in Holmes's direction, staring straight into his eyes. — For the sake of obtaining information, you ready to sell even your own mother. All of you are the same.

■ Look. — Holmes showed Tyutkin the expert estimation of the value of the jewelry that was seized after Tyrin's death.

Tyutkin carefully studied the document. It seemed he had come back to life. After reading the document, his voice changed. He talked as an absolutely healthy, sane person. Not a single sign of the disease was visible. For a split second, it seemed to me he had significant experience in theatrical art and showed an excellent actor's play.

■ So, it means in vain I didn't believe him. — Tyutkin continued the conversation. — He warned me. — Anton swore. — Then, three years ago, someone killed Tyrin's guard in my house. He was with the bandits. That's why I concluded about Tyrin's involvement in the incident.

■ Was anyone else of the bandits killed?

■ No. Only him.

■ Did you use the weapon? Who killed him?

■ I don't know. We were sleeping when they attacked. My wife and I didn't understand at once what was happening. The group of robbers stood before us. They demanded to open the safe. — Anton fiddled the duvet cover by his fingers. — I pretended to obey and led them to my office. Two bandits followed me. The rest of them scattered around the house. Probably, then the wife secretly called our daughter. Lydia could escape and called to the police. For this, the robbers killed my wife.

■ Did the shootout start after the police arrive?

■ Yes. As soon as we heard approaching to the house the sirens of the police cars, they started beating me.

■ What did they steal from the safe?

- I did not have time to open it. Out of the fear, I've forgotten where I put the key and could not find it. It made them angry.
- How many robbers were there?
- Five in our bedroom. When we were walking to the study, I saw others. Because of fear, I could not count them.
- Don't you consider it's strange? There were many robbers inside your house. They stole nothing, and only one person was killed — Tyrin's guard.
- Then I didn't think about it. It was enough for me to see Tyrin's man among the robbers to understand who hired them.
- Usually the person cannot think rationally in the stressful situation like yours. He sees what he wants to see or what someone wants this person to see.
- Now, after learning the truth about Tyrin, I don't presume to argue with you. — Anton tilted his head down a little and rubbed the back of his neck. — Maybe it really was Brazilian wanderer, as Tyrin said.
- Do you know him? Who is he?
- I only know that this is a virtual type who bought all the Atlantis's artifacts.
- Probably it will be better if you tell the entire story. First tell me, did Tyrin's guard have the tattoo on his wrist?
- Yes. A crossed sword and a broom are inside an eight-pointed star. They are entwined with a rose. I noticed it, because my guard has the same tattoo. I asked him what's the meaning of it. He said: it's modern.
- Really? Where is your guard now?
- I don't know. He quit the job a month ago.
- Okay. Let's start from the beginning: how did you meet Tyrin and from when your joined work began?
- I met Tyrin in my youth when I studied at the Odessa College of Finance. We had the same age and studied in the same group. After college, he entered the law faculty of the Odessa Law Academy. I

continued to study finance at the Odessa Institute of Trade and Economics. We corresponded for a long time after graduation. Then our paths parted. I returned to my hometown of Nikolayev. He got a job in a law firm in Kiev. Our correspondence narrowed down to sending greeting cards to significant and festive dates. But nine years ago he came to me in Nikolayev. Then, I kept a small cafe in the center of the city. Soon he offered me to open galleries in Odessa. Tyrin told me about his business. A year before our meeting, he was appointed as an ambassador to Spain. He was lucky to meet one person who told him about sunken ships with jewelry off the coast of the island of Cabrera. Cabrera is part of the Balearic Islands. Tyrin was born and raised in Odessa. As you know, people from Odessa are smart. He found in Odessa two scuba divers with experience and offered them a job. Officially, they worked in a cafe on the island of Cabrera. In their free time, they searched for sunken ships. But it was not so easy. Abroad they treat work very responsibly. Two days a week was not enough for hunting the treasure. Tyrin already had a small ship and two divers' suits, which allows to dive a little over 300 meters. The man from Odessa managed the ship. In order not to attract special attention, Tyrin had to hire two more people, but from Nikolayev. The scuba divers, he had hired before, recommended them. So they worked alternately for about half a year. Finally, the fortune turned the face on them. One day they discovered a ship at a depth of 70 meters. They found a huge number of the ancient amphorae there. Most amphorae were up to -one-meter high. The ship looked completely untouched from the moment of flooding. In order to determine the value of the find, Tyrin sent an amphora to his friend for examination. The expert was from Russia. But he worked in Spain in an archaeological group. The main Tyrin's feature, he easily entered communication with people and selected acquaintance for any occasion. He knew people well. According to his expert, these amphorae date back to the 3rd or 4th century AD. As a specialist in this field, he clearly identified that such vessels were built in North Africa. It was the beginning of the artifacts' selling. His friend introduced him to a man who had access to the black auctions. It lasted a little over three years. During this time, they discovered seven more ships. One of them was from the time of the Roman Empire. They found dishes from Chinese porcelain from the Ming Dynasty, smoking pipes, and much more from household utensils on the ships. But for the last half a year, someone has found out about Tyrin's business and has taken up with it. The first time Tyrin paid off. But subsequent times this person demanded more and more money for the silence. Tyrin's patience burst and he announced to the press about his find. The Spanish government even paid him the bonus for it. During this time, he has already made a good fortune. I turned into the wealthy person too. Tyrin gave me 20 percent of sales, the scuba divers received 5 percent and Murzyan — 10 percent. Tyrin got 50 percent of sales. But no one argued. All equipment belonged to Tyrin. He also organized the working process. It was clear he had to bribe to various officials for silence and help in transporting the artifacts.

■ How could he transport such things through the customs?

■ Basically, he used the captains of the ships to send the goods to the different countries of the world. To Ukraine, he was transporting the artifacts in his luggage. Ambassador's suitcases are not checked at customs. Sometimes he returned to Odessa by his ship. But in Ukraine there are a few rich people who are interested in ancient artifacts. Most of the buyers were from the foreign countries.

■ To the people of which country, did you mainly sell your product?

■ Tyrin did not tell me about it, because he could not know. At the black auction, only nicknames are visible, not the person's real name. It was not important. The principal thing for us was to send the goods and get the money. Before the announcing about finding sunk ships, Tyrin bought the deep-sea vehicle "Russ". He dreamed of exploring the great depths of the Mediterranean Sea. Then his dream was not destined to come true, and it upset him. The bathyscaphe cost a lot of money. So, our activity has stopped. But after a little more than a year, he was transferred as ambassador to Cyprus. I must tell you, he loved to search through the Internet for sensational finds of antiquity. Before his transfer to Cyprus, someone posted a photo of the coin there. By all indications, it was like the monetary unit of Atlantis. Despite various refutations under this photo that this is a fake, Tyrin checked it. He wrote to the respondent about being interested in his find. In the letter he offered to buy the coin. Thus began their correspondence. The guy was from Cyprus. Tyrin flew on the meeting with him. After this meeting, he was appointed as ambassador to Cyprus. He didn't start the search for Atlantis at once. The first question was: how to transport a bathyscaphe to Cyprus. The second question was related to the first - where to moor it. Tyrin spent almost a month to resolve these problems. He became acquainted with the head of the port of Paphos. As a result, Tyrin signed an agreement with him for the parking of his small ship and bathyscaphe "Russ". I have little knowledge of this technique and worried about how Tyrin will use them. In my understanding, we need a ship for transferring the bathyscaphe to the place where the sea is deep. Only after it, the bathyscaphe can plunge into the water. The achievement of technological progress surprised me. It turned out, this bathyscaphe himself could move under water. This simplified the matter. The bathyscaphe itself takes on board a crew of three people, which can be there up to 12 hours. The device can dive to a depth of over 6,000 meters. Its capabilities exceeded our needs, since the maximum depth of the Mediterranean Sea is just over five thousand meters. While Tyrin was looking for connections, Murzyan studied how to manage the bathyscaphe. When he sailed on a ship, two scuba divers helped him. He himself would not have done it. The case with the bathyscaphe was different. Tyrin demanded only Murzyan to learn how to navigate the bathyscaphe under water and how to control it. He announced this information as the confidential, and no one can know it. Tyrin trusted Murzyan because he was friends with Murzyan's father.

- If Tyrin was friends with Murzyan's father, how could he kill his son?
- Tyrin did not kill him. Murzyan himself ran into a stray knife with his show off. But let's all in order so as not to confuse. According to the agreement between a man from Cyprus and Tyrin, the crew of the bathyscaphe included Cypriot. He was about twenty-five years old, and was born in the city of Kouklia, which is near Paphos. The Cypriot's father visited them about a week after the start of our expedition. It was the evening, and they recently returned from the searching. Our men lived in the same house. Two people in a room. Cypriot shared the room with Murzyan. His father was indignant. It looked like he wanted to take his son home by force. They even had a fight with each other. This quarrel didn't lead them to the compromise, and his father went home alone. Murzyan asked the guy what happened. Cypriot told the strange story. The Cypriots believe in one ancient legend. The entire civilization immersed in the water. It was about Atlantis. According to this legend, God forbade to look for this island. He punished the people from the island for their grave sins by immersing their civilization in the depths of the sea. They violated the traditions, transmitted by their ancestors, and lost the moral qualities which they originally endowed with. Degradation occurred. It led to the decline of the entire Atlantis empire. If anyone dares to look for Atlantis, the God's punishment will befall him. Just as the sea waves swallowed Atlantis, so a naughty person will suffer sudden death.

Murzyan told this story to scuba divers. At first, fear constrained everyone. There was no desire to climb into the unknown, which will bring nothing but death. Tyrin reacted calmly. He did not believe in this legend and considered it simple prejudices. So another week

129

passed. Atlantis was not found. Cypriot said that he found coins on the seashore. It is hard to say how the coins appeared from the depths of the sea. This is not a bottle with the letter. But the fact remains. At last the wished day came. The bathyscaphe hooked something heavy with his manipulator. It turned out to be a horse's head. Because it was hard to distinguish from which material the sculpture was made of, they returned to the port. For examining the statue, they had to wait until sunset. When the find was raised to the surface and cleaned of silt and dirt, it became obvious — they had found Atlantis. The horse's head was part of a sculpture. According to Plato, the six flying horses were harnessed in chariot which stood in a temple in the center of Atlantis. It delighted everyone. From time to time, goosebumps walked along of admired adventurers when they recalled the warning from a legend. No wonder there is a saying: the greed killed dude. This happened in our case. The first affected Cypriot. After the horse's head, they found a chest of money. They immediately divided the money in a percentage ratio, which was initially agreed upon with Tyrin. As for the horse's head, they postponed the section until we sold it.

That day, our researchers went to sea late, because there was a strong wind and the storm. Murzyan offered to rest all day. So they did. By evening the storm had subsided, and they went to make the researching even if it takes a couple of hours. They returned late after sunset. Cypriot wanted wine and went straight to the store. Murzyan tried to stop him, but apparently it was time for the warning to come true. The researchers came home and waited for Cypriot there, but in vain. Then they went to search for him. They knew the place where he always went for wine. It was a small cozy bar which was five hundred meters from their house. Cypriot was not there. They began asking guests of the cafe and workers. One server said he had seen him to go towards the sea. They headed in that direction. When they were already on the shore, there was a crowd of people and the police there. Our men went to see what caused the crowd to gather. It was a terrifying view. The dead Cypriot was lying on the sand. Witnesses said that he went to the breakwater. There he slipped and fell on his back. He probably hit his head hard, because when he got up he was staggering. People ran to help him, but he staggered and fell into the sea. Because of darkness, they did not find him right away. When they got him, he was already dead, drowned in the water.

Seeing the lifeless body of the Cypriot, our researchers remembered the warning from an ancient legend. According to Murzyan's words, his hair stood on end. They had feelings like someone had poured a tub of ice water on them. The police took the corpse for autopsy. Our men could not call his parents, because they did not have their phone number. The police called them. Tyrin sent the money to Cypriot's parents, but they refused to take it, because the money was earned by the illegal way.

About a week, the group did not go to sea. At the weekend, Tyrin arrived. He persuaded the team to stop believing in superstition. According to Tyrin, the Cypriot suffered such a fate, since he believed in it. If you do not believe in it, then this will not happen. Little by little, somehow everything calmed down. On Wednesday, the second week after the incident, the team went to sea. They were lucky. They raised from the bottom of the sea a statue of Nereid sitting on a dolphin. Then small household utensils as tea cups, plates and the like came across. Our adventurers perked up. Selling the statue brought a lot of money. We could have stopped already, but human greed is insatiable. No one even thought to stop. The daily finds encouraged us. Then they found the wing of some creature and the pair of scrolls made of gold. About half a year later, they raised from the seabed the second statue of Nereid sitting on a dolphin. It has been almost eight months since they worked in the area of sunken Atlantis. After the finding the second statue, Tyrin visited the adventurers. Usually he didn't miss an opportunity to come to them on the weekend, but then, it was a weekday. He announced he doesn't want to put up this statue for sale. According to his explanation, he didn't want to draw special attention to the finds. Tyrin offered to transport the statue to my house and put it in a room near the back exit. For this aim I ordered the manufacture of a special partition that hid the statue from unnecessary eyes. Without knowing the layout of the rooms in my house, no one could guess that the room should be larger. It was the reason the robbers did not find her three years ago. Tyrin transported the statue himself. Even before his arrival, I had the impression that he was afraid of something. You won't ask this on the phone. He arrived with the statue in the evening and stayed overnight. After supper, my wife and daughter went to their rooms. We stayed alone and drank wine on the terrace. It was great an opportunity to ask him about my suspicions. And to my great regret, I was right. I'll retell you his story.

When Tyrin put up for auction the statue Nereid sitting on a dolphin, an American museum became interested in the statue and bought it for $1 billion. A fabulous price. In order to take part in a legal auction, we found a sculptor-drunkard in Odessa. He agreed to help us. No one expected him to tell about the statue of the head of a flying horse which was in my gallery on Deribasovskaya. Some politician from Ukraine became interested in this exhibit. His name was strictly classified. According to his demand, I have to sell this statue on the black auction to Brazilian wanderer. I cannot explain to you how he found out about our deals, but we fulfilled his demand.

- How could you document what was sold at a black auction?
- It turned out to be very easy. The American museum has sent a request to purchase an exhibit. We entered an official contract for the import of goods, and I sent the statue to America.
- At what price?

- The cost of the statue corresponded to my net profit after deducting all taxes, including dividends.
- It's interesting. What about the sum which Tyrin and his team have to receive?
- Tyrin received the money on his account in the offshore bank.
- Okay. Continue.
- We sold little in the Ukrainian market. Scuba divers and Murzyan sometimes haggled in Odessa and other big cities of Ukraine, but this was not a constant market. Basically, everything depended on Tyrin and his participation in black auctions. From this time, no matter in which auctions he took part, Brazilian wanderer always appeared there. Despite of price, he was offering a bigger sum for exhibits that no one could beat. He bought all our artifacts. Just a month before finding the second statue of Nereid, Tyrin received the letter on his email-box from Brazilian wanderer. This shocked and alerted Tyrin. To take part in the auction, Tyrin chose the nickname Elusive Firefly. At the auction, people always used nicknames. No one knew the real names, not to mention email addresses. The buyers transferred the money to the organizer of the auction, and he already was sending it to the sellers. Basically, for such purposes, the auction's participants opened the settlement accounts in the banks in offshore zones. The organizer of the auction was also the founder and the director of such a bank. They thought the schemes out to the smallest detail. No one could find out either the name of the person or where he opened the current account. Tyrin has opened the accounts in different countries. And here is such an extraordinary situation. As I said earlier, Tyrin had a unique ability to find contacts with the right people and negotiate. People trusted him. I've never heard he betrayed someone. But three years ago he has changed and sent the thieves to my house.
- Perhaps he did not betray you.
- You are again for yours.

- We'll summarize after all your story. Now please continue.
- So here. Brazilian wanderer demanded Tyrin to open a place of the extraction of artifacts, otherwise he threatened a general exposure to the public. Tyrin was not afraid of it. He designed everything legally. In Cyprus, he registered a study group of five. He was the customer of such studies. He owned the ship and the bathyscaphe. According to the documents, Tyrin hired people for studying the seafloor reliefs and search for underwater secrets hidden from the human's eyes. He also bribed a senior official and was giving him part of the profits from the sales. The official was satisfied and made no complaints. In order to expose our group, it is necessary to catch our men red-handed. This is difficult. I thought we have a snitch among the researchers. But all worked as one. Still Tyrin miscalculated. I'll tell more on this subject later. Tyrin wrote the claim to the organizer of the last auction, and he quickly received the answer from him. He confirmed that a month ago Brazilian wanderer asked for information about Tyrin. He refused to provide it. After his refusal, the local authorities ordered to check his bank. The auction's organizer laid on the bottom and does not organize auctions. This man warned Tyrin that three years ago there were rumors about appearance of some dishonest player. This player bought goods from one person and later took his entire business. His acquaintance, who lost thus his business, was afraid to name the nickname of his pursuer. As you see, this information has surfaced by itself. His name is Brazilian wanderer. Based on the practice, we concluded that Tyrin's fate is a foregone conclusion. He needs to do something in order not to give up the business. Not always things happen the way you want or plan. Soon Tyrin ordered to suspend the researching and all team return home to Ukraine. Two scuba divers flew home by plane. Tyrin moved the bathyscaphe from Cyprus to the Illichivsk port. It remains only to transport the remaining artifacts. They turned out to be quite a few. Tyrin agreed with the captain of the

Chinese ship to transport his belongings. He did not disclose what it was, but paid generously. The captain did not ask. They agreed that in neutral waters near Ukraine, they will reload the cargo to Tyrin's ship. To fulfill this mission, Murzyan and two scuba divers had to return home on Tyrin's ship.

Tyrin took a vacation and flew home by plane. Things went swimmingly. They reloaded cargo without problems, and Tyrin's ship sailed home. You know he has a good pier. When Murzyan was three miles from Tyrin's house, he saw a police boat was drifting into the sea. The presence of the police boat did not take his attention. They keep order, and we can often see them at sea. But when Murzyan were about a mile from Tyrin's pier, other police boats appeared from all directions. Our men got scared. It was obvious the police were surrounding Tyrin's ship. Running away was not where, and it was useless. The documents show whose ship is. So the police arrested all four: Tyrin, Murzyan and two scuba divers.

Later it turned out that at the same time the police arrested two other scuba divers. They took them to a pre-trial detention center and put in a separate cell. It looked like someone has planned the arrest in advance. But by whom? That's the question. The police made the mistake of putting the first four prisoners in the same room. They had time to discuss what had happened and to think about how to get out of the situation. According to the legislation of Ukraine, for the concealment and misappropriation of ancient artifacts, a fine in the amount of 1,700 to 2,550 hryvnias can be imposed. The police can involve the culprits in community service or corrective labor. The maximum punishment under this article of the criminal code is arrest for up to 6 months. Having discussed all the possible worst options in the current situation, they concluded that there is no need to worry. This is not the worst thing which can be in this life. Murzyan offered to lie that he and scuba divers found the treasure in Bulgaria. When they sailed home from Cyprus, they went to the Bulgarian resort "Sunny Beach". Mostly in the evening at the resort, people visit the casinos and the night bars. Our men were not an exception. They spent their last day in a nightclub. There Murzyan met a man who told him about the treasure. The man was very drunk, and his story seemed ridiculous. Because he spent money left and right on thoughtlessly, this prompted Murzyan to check the veracity of the story. The treasure was in the cemetery in one crypt. Alexius offered the scuba divers a night walk. They agreed. So they had two large suitcases with treasures in their hands. Tyrin knew nothing about it at all. According to an agreement between Murzyan and Tyrin, Alexius could use Tyrin's ship when he needed. For this, Tyrin received income from the renting. Everything is official. In fact, there was income, and Tyrin declared it in the annual declaration. He paid taxes to the budget from this income. They agreed to use this story. But it didn't work out as planned. Their wonderful plan burst like a soap bubble. The interrogation began from Tyrin, and the first question stunned him. The detective asked: "Where is the location of Atlantis?". Tyrin's breath caught. In a few seconds he regained consciousness. The detective repeated the question. Tyrin denied everything. He swore, knowing nothing about the treasure. This is all the work of Murzyan. Tyrin only leased his ship to him. And where he sailed and what he found, Tyrin had no idea. The detective was not satisfied with an answer. He threatened Tyrin with dismissal from the post of ambassador. Tyrin was ready for this and took the threat calmly. He demanded the lawyer. After his demand, Tyrin exercised his right to silence. He wanted to get back to the cell as soon as possible and tell his employees what was happening. But this was not destined to happen. The police put him in another cell. Tyrin did not see his subordinates until the moment of his release. When the lawyer got involved, things went quicker. Tyrin could convey the message to his acquaintance, thanks to whom he advanced up the career ladder. This acquaintance worked in the presidential administration and had tremendous connections and influence. Tyrin shared money with him, and he always covered him. He helped him this time too, but it took five days. At last Tyrin was released. His acquaintance contacted him via Skype. They considered it's the safest way to negotiate. According to his explanation, a very influential person is hunting Tyrin. His goal is to find out the location of Atlantis. If Tyrin reveals this information, a powerful person will allow him to live. But the acquaintance warned Tyrin that this was not a fact. He knows this person, and he has never heard he even once left his victim alive. After a while the victim dies, anyway. Hearing this information, Tyrin wrote a letter of resignation himself and laid low. His friend supported this decision. So Tyrin quit his job and indulged in entertainment. He became a gambler who squandered his entire fortune in a year. Immediately after his dismissal, Tyrin hired a bodyguard who was with him 24 hours a day. The bodyguard was killed during the attack on my house. From this time on, Tyrin hired no one. He was as poor as a church mouse. Now I understand it was his maneuver to survive. Then it looked exactly as I am telling it.

Immediately after his release, Tyrin looked for his subordinates. But only in a month he found them. To his horror, four scuba divers were in Mariupol psychiatric hospital, and the court put Murzyan in prison for 10 years. Thanks to his connections, Tyrin could find out what had happened. All began from the police announcement about Tyrin's betrayal, as if he was released and left them behind. First, his subordinates did not believe in the police statement. They were convinced in his promise and waited that he will soon achieve their release. But day after day passed, and no one heard of him. Not getting what they wanted with the help of persuasion and threats, the police began to beat the scuba divers and Murzyan, sometimes very severely. The police transferred them to some special bunker without windows and placed in the different single cells. Our adventurers were in cells without light. In the gloomy darkness, they lost track of time and days. Every patience ends. Being in this position, they gave up. The divers were the first who spoke. They told everything what they knew, but they could not tell the major point: the path to the Atlantis's location. Only Tyrin and Murzyan knew about it. After such a statement, the police were beating Alexius even harder. But a person who has completed military service in the navy is not so easy to break. He was silent or told the story about the Bulgarian resort. From being in the dark and constant beatings, the scuba divers went crazy. Murzyan was beaten so much that he could not rise and hardly breath. Then the police officers received an order to place the scuba divers in the Mariupol psychiatric hospital, and Murzyan — in prison, because of accusation of hiding secrets of state significance.

To arrange the meeting with Murzyan, Tyrin bribed the chief of the prison. Finally, the long-awaited meeting day has come, but Alexius refused to see him. According to the guards, he did not want to meet with Tyrin. Tyrin went there again and again. You can guess how much money he spent to have approval on these meetings. In five months, Georgy resigned himself to the fact that Murzyan did not want to hear the truth. Tyrin came to me a month after his last visit to the prison. He looked upset and complained of pain in the heart's region. He had grown older and thinner. Tyrin could not accept to the undeserved punishment of his subordinates. He suffered a lot because he could not help them. We went to Mariupol together. If I tell you, the sight was terrible, I told nothing. The four scuba divers were insane. Sometimes consciousness returned to them. Such periods were not long. About a month before the attempted robbery of my house, Tyrin called me. He said that Murzyan's wife came to him and asked for help. Alexius was ill. She didn't tell what the disease was. Tyrin immediately drove to the prison. This time Alexius agreed to have a meeting. The prison guard showed Tyrin a meeting room. The meeting took place in the presence of a security guard. Murzyan looked disgusting. His pale face showed a serious illness. He complained of headaches and hallucinations. Tyrin persuaded him to meet with a lawyer. Surprisingly, Alexius agreed. A day later, Tyrin went to the prison with a lawyer. They wrote an appeal to review the case. After meeting with Murzyan, Tyrin with the lawyer drove to the court and registered the application. Now they demanded to see the evidence that testified to Murzyan's concealment of secrets of state importance. The court's clerk promised to give them the case in the afternoon on the next day. But nobody went to the court for learning the case's materials. It was almost the midday when the lawyer called to Tyrin with news about Murzyan's death. From surprise, Tyrin's heart could not stand it. He went to hospital with a pre-infarction condition.

When I saw the killed Tyrin's guard, the doubts disappeared by themselves. I knew who arranged the outrage in my mansion. The next day, all the newspapers were full of the articles about the attack on my house. The internet was not the exception. In the evening he dared to call me and asked what happened. Such a hypocrite. I cursed him and told not to call me again, never ever.

- ■ According to your words, you cursed him. I heard you told to Tyrin that you hid the statue under the pool.
- ■ Me? No. I didn't do it.
- ■ Really? Hm. Okay. In my opinion Brazilian wanderer staged the robbery of your house.
- ■ Come on. What does he care about me? If you compare my share and Tyrin's share, you'll understand who Brazilian wanderer desired to get. How could he know I have jewelry? I have told no one about it. You've forgotten, I have my business which unrelated to the Tyrin's.
- ■ Is it so? - Holmes narrowed his eyes and carefully examined Anton. — Your daughter is wearing a coin necklace for show. These coins are

artifacts from Atlantis. And you forgot one more thing: the statue. You have hidden in your house the statue of Nereid sitting on a dolphin. Most likely they came for her. When did you hire your guard?

- About five years ago.
- Did you get now how Brazilian wanderer found out about statue?
- I can agree with you about their coming for the statue. But why are you sure it was Brazilian Wanderer's plan?
- You saw a tattoo on the wrist of Tyrin's guard and yours. This is not a simple tattoo. It indicates that a person belongs to a particular group. Brazilian wanderer leads this group in Ukraine.
- My driver has the same tattoo.
- With which I congratulate you. What the hospital's department is your driver in?
- We discharged him yesterday. — The doctor intervened in the conversation.
- How can it be? — Tyutkin asked with disbelieving voice. His eyebrows lifted, and the widening eyes seemed going to pop out of their sockets. — The thieves severely beat him. How could he heal so quickly?
- He had nothing terrible. A couple of bruises on the body, a black eye and a split lip. These are all his injuries.
- It cannot be. — Anton raised his voice. — I saw how severely they beat him. I highly recommend you to check him more carefully. He may have damage to internal organs. The thieves were beating him in the stomach and the spine with feet.
- Upon admission to the hospital, he underwent a complete examination. He had no serious injuries.
- Doesn't that tell you anything? — Holmes asked, gazing directly at Anton's eyes.

Tyutkin fell silent. He lowered his head and hunched. Then began fingering the duvet cover. It looked like he was thinking about something unpleasant. Suddenly he raised his head.

- I'll call him and order to come straight away to me. — Anton dialed the number. We heard as the voice said this number is not on service. He hung up. — Okay. He has to be at the office. — He called again. His secretary took the call. Anton switched on the speakerphone. — Where is Ilya?
- At the hospital.
- The doctor said he discharged him yesterday. Find him and order to come to me at once. — Anton hung up.
- Don't waste your time and energy. — Holmes said. — You will not find him. Let's return to our sheep. Why did you say Murzyan himself ran into a stray knife with his show off?
- Because it's the truth. When Tyrin visited him and told about the lawyer, Alexius was talking freely about Atlantis. He threatened Tyrin that he will tell to someone the location of Atlantis after his release. If he said it to Tyrin, surely he could say it to the prisoners.
- Hm. That's interesting. Didn't Alexius look like he used drugs?
- Tyrin suspected it, but his wife said he had a flu. According to Alexius's wife, he had a high temperature.
- In my opinion, Tyrin was right. The answer on the question, why Alexius refused to meet Tyrin and his wife, is simple. They didn't allow to him to have a meeting. You told they have beaten him severely that he even could not rise and walk. If his wife saw him then, what would she do? Right. She would have filed the complaint to the court. Its obvious someone powerful from the prison works with criminals. It means they tried to find out the needed information. How they could do it? They trained him to drugs. Under the drugs, he could have lost control and tell them the secret.
- You can be right. Did he tell them the secret?
- Who knows? Looking how they easily killed Tyrin, it's possible. Who hired the lawyer for Alexius? His wife of Tyrin?

■ His wife. She said the lawyer promised to release Alexius during one year.

■ Okay. One more things. Someone killed the thieves who robbed you. — Holmes turned to the doctor and asked. — May I show Anton their photos to identify?

■ No. He cannot …

■ I can. — Tyutkin interrupted the doctor and continued with commander voice. — Give me the photos. I want to see them.

■ Okay. I'll inject him the sedative. — The doctor made the injection. — Show him only the faces without wounds. The medicine needs a time to work.

Holmes obeyed the doctor's demand. He picked up from the bag the photos, sorted five of them and handed to Tyutkin. Looking at the first and second photo, Anton recognized no one. He said with irritation:

■ Who do you want me to recognize? A? — Tyutkin gave Holmes dismissive look and said angrily. —Do you think if two people of the criminal gang worked in my company, I know all their representatives?

■ Certainly not. I presume your guard took part in the robbery.

■ Come on, Holmes. — He sharply threw the viewed photos away from him and continued the viewing. His face became red. — You want to tell you are penetrating?

■ No. I want just to check my assumption. — Holmes said in a calm tone. — That's all.

■ What's this? — He turned the fourth photo towards us. — Do you have the other photo where I can distinguish the face clearly?

Holmes looked at the photos again, chose two of them and handed to Tyutkin. Anton grabbed the photos and began studying them carefully. He brought the photographs closer to his face and squinted his eyes as if trying to distinguish something better there. He pushed them further away from him and brought them closer again.

■ Did you recognize your security guard in the photo and can't believe it? — Holmes asked.

Tyutkin did not answer. I'm not sure if he even heard the question. He was engulfed in his thoughts. Suddenly he woke up from the dream and was looking around with a blank look like didn't understand where he was and what's going on here. Then he fixed his gaze on Holmes. This went on for several minutes before he spoke.

■ Yes. This is the photo of my security guard. — He said with irritation. — Do you satisfy?

■ Not really. You confirmed my assumption, but it did not help me in resolving the question of who killed them and why. Let's go back to our investigation. Two scuba divers visited you. What were you talking about?

■ They wanted to take their share. When they got out of the hospital, they went straight to Tyrin. He sent them to me. I told you, when the police arrested Tyrin and Murzyan with scuba divers, they confiscated all jewelry. After Tyrin's release, he allocated to the scuba divers and Murzyan their portion from his reserves. He brought the scuba divers' jewelry to me for storage. What he prepared for Murzyan, he gave to his wife. They came to me less than a month ago. I promised to take the jewelry from the bank and to give them what I owe. My health was poor, and I asked for postpone fulfilling an agreement. Because they had nowhere to hide, I allowed them to live in the attic of one of my restaurants. I introduced the scuba divers to my deputy as my friend's relatives and ordered to feed them well. So they had a roof over their heads and food. I gave them money too. Because the police were looking for them, they could not go outside freely. Sometimes they went for a walk, but only in the late evening.

■ Did you notify the scuba divers about thieves' attack? Where did you agree to meet for transferring the jewelry?

- In my house. When I was robbed, they were waiting for me in the car near my mansion. I immediately informed them of the incident. And they chased the bandits.
- Have you taken all the jewelry from the bank?
- Unfortunately, yes.
- Do you have their phone number?
- Sure. I'll look now. — Tyutkin took his phone and looked for the information.
- Did they take the jewels from the bandits?
- I don't know. They didn't call to me. Here it is.
- Didn't they tell to you about their plan? — Holmes was asking and writing at the same time. — Weren't they going to leave the country?
- We had no time for conversation, because they were in a great hurry.
- Don't you mind if we make a call from your telephone?
- May I call them myself? - Tyutkin took his phone from Holmes and called. We heard beeps. Someone picked up the phone. Holmes turned on the speakerphone.
- It was in vain we didn't listen to his parents' warning. — The man's voice said from the tube. — The curse from the ancient legend works. Now you remained alone. Beware!
- What's up? — Tyutkin's eyebrows lifted. His eyes were widening. — Where are you? Did you take the jewelry from the bandits?
- It would be better if we took your money and left. We would have stayed alive. — We heard a shot accompanied by a triumphant laugh. Then there was a splash of water, as if something big had been dropped into it. — Vadim is dead. Nobody will get the jewelry. — These words were accompanied by sound, as if a lot of the small objects were dropping into the water.
- Where are you? — Anton began to shake. He continued to speak, stammering. — What happened?

- Goodbye. Now it's my ... — The second shot interrupted the man's conversation. We heard as the phone was falling into the water. The connection was interrupted.
- What was it? — His nervous condition caused facial tics. He looked at us without blinking.
- The scuba divers were killed.
- Killed? — He shouted. The face became red. — By whom?
- People, who robbed you, are from the gang of Brazilian wanderer. The police gave me the criminal case of their murder investigation, and I studied the materials of the autopsy with photographs. All the men had tattoos on their wrists. The scuba diver told the truth. It would be better if they took the money from you and did not mess with this criminal organization. Apparently they didn't know who they faced. Because of this, they thought killing thieves will lead to the end of the game. But instead of getting the freedom, they have provoked the beginning of the hunt.
- Who reported to the gang that the scuba divers killed their men? How could they trace the scuba divers?
- Elementary. After the attack, you called to the scuba divers. Your driver was with you and heard the conversation.
- Oh. — Tyutkin fell into the thought. In a few seconds, he continued. — But still. How did Brazilian wanderer know about the day I was going to collect the jewelry from the bank?
- Your driver is from their gang. — Holmes reminded to Anton, looking directly at his eyes.
- Only my daughter knew about it. When we had a conversation, the driver was not around.
- To what extent is Tyutkin at risk of a second nervous breakdown now? — Holmes asked the doctor. — This concerns his daughter.

The doctor looked at his watch. After a few seconds, he nodded and said:

■ The sedative has to work now. Let's try. I'll watch him. If his condition became worse, I'll stop you.

■ Good. — Holmes turned to Tyutkin. — What do your words mean: "Now all will be okay, I will be avenged"?

■ My daughter said that she was going to meet Tyrin. She was planning to rob him.

■ And you reacted calmly to this? Don't you think she might get hurt?

■ Then I was angry with him and did not think about it.

Holmes took out his phone. He opened Lydia's correspondence with a man from America and gave to Tyutkin.

■ Read on what you blessed your daughter for. To some extent, you are responsible for her death, because you did not stop her.

Tyutkin read in silence. His face became pale. Hands trembling became noticeable. Tears rolled from his eyes. When he finished reading, he looked like a mortally wounded animal.

■ So, it was all planned by someone. — His voice sounded like he was in trance. He raised his head and looked at us with a wandering gaze. — We fell on the hook of this manipulator and killed an innocent person. - The shame and the horror at the same time sounded in his words. We saw in him as if the other man was looking at us by Tyutkin's eyes. This information destroyed him to the ground. — How can I live with this now? — He stretched out his hands to us as if looking for a guide. Then he covered his face with his hands.

■ After the treatment, answer for what you did. One sage said: one must be able to live even when life becomes unbearable. Maybe it will console you. God gave you the life, and you must live. Think how you can atone for your sins before God. Goodbye.

With these words Holmes left the room. I and Ruslan followed him. In short time the doctor joined us. We thanked for his help and said goodbye.

Chapter XVII: Did God curse atlantes?

I felt unpleasant sediment, some dissatisfaction in my soul. Perhaps this is an excellent student's syndrome. I don't like the fact that we again lost to this nasty spider. At last, we came outside the building.

- Thank you for your great help. — Holmes said to Ruslan. — This is the end of the mission. Give our thanks to your team. We are going home.
- Mycroft ordered to escort you to Kiev.
- It's too much.
- I don't think so. We have seriously angered the criminal group. Besides, an order is an order. I cannot disobey.

Holmes had nothing to say. Ruslan was right. The criminal group lost Tyrin's artifacts, blow up the statue from the Atlantis, lost the Tyutkin's treasure. In the addition they killed the last person who knew the location of Atlantis. So we hit the road home. Ruslan's car was driving ahead of us. His second car joined us at the exit from Nikolayev. It was really an escort. The mood was lousy. Holmes was sitting next to me in the back seat of the car. Steve was driving. Holmes rested his elbow on the car's door and rested his head on his hand. He was looking into the distance. Did he see something there, or was he lost in thought? I interrupted his thoughts.

- Do you think God really cursed the atlantes?
- I cannot say this for sure, but if they departed from the commandments of God and turned into a corrupted herd of animals, then He could well punish them as Sodom and Gomorrah. God destroyed the inhabitants of these cities for their sins and, in particular, for debauchery.
- You are talking about a Christian God. Plato wrote the atlantes worshiped Poseidon, the god of the sea. According to his writing, they flourished as long as they kept the ancient commandments. When they began to live as they pleased, their island had sunken into the depths of the sea.
- Believe it or not, all people are descendants of Adam and Eve. Darwin tried hard in his evolution to describe the origin of man from ape. Personally, I don't believe in it. There is a parable as a scientist argued with God that he could do what God does. To this, God said to him: "You will prove to me your ability if you create a man." The scientist replied: "Good." He bent down to take the dust of the earth, but God stopped him. He told the scientist: "No. You create your earthly dust, but don't touch mine."
- Ha-ha-ha. — Steve burst into laughter. — You are something, Holmes. I've never heard it before. It's an outstanding example for pointing person at his place under the sun.

After that, the situation was defused, and the atmosphere was no longer so dull and tense. But I was bursting with questions. And Holmes did not mind. Sometimes his patience amazes me.

- About Poseidon. It is inherent in man to deify what he cannot understand. Read the Bible. When Moses went to meet with God and returned after a sometime, the people of Israel made a golden calf and worshiped him. What prevented the atlantes from doing the same? They lived on an island surrounded by water. There is nothing surprising in this. One man checked, will human deify the unknown.

He closed his child in the room and has never told him about God. When the child became older, the father found his son was praying to the sun.

- As far as I know, the atlantes were giants.
- The Bible also mentions giants many times. We can find the information about them in the history of many nations, the legends and folk tales.
- From where did they come? I heard the story they appeared after the human women had affairs with the sons of God. Here, under the sons of God, meant Angels.
- There are two understandings of the text of the Bible who are the sons of God. According to the first version, the Angels lived with the daughters of men. As a result, from their cohabitation, the women began to birth to giants. But the Lord said that Angels do not marry. They live a sexless, non-carnal life, and therefore they cannot do this. Only people can do this. The second version, the sons of God, are the descendants of Seth. He with his family were the first, who arranged the divine service. They kept the faith on earth. Ephraim the Syrian says, the sons of God were giants, and the Cainites were small people. As you know, their father Cain killed his brother. God cursed him and his family. When the sons of God began to live with the women from the Cainites, the women also gave birth to giants. The women corrupted the men who served God. It was the beginning of their falling. Before the flood, people lived up to a thousand years. The giants were healthy and beautiful people. Longevity and the above listed qualities turned their heads. They thought they were gods. The giants became arrogant, very cocky. This was the birth of all wickedness, vice, and blasphemy. The giants stopped worshiping God and worshipped themselves as gods. Because of this, God brought a flood and everything living on earth perished. Of the people, only righteous Noah and his family survived.

- Good. But it was before the flood. Where did the giants come from after the flood, if only Noah and his family were alive?

- According to the patristic opinion that the sons of God were giants. From this we can conclude: because Noah was a descendant of Seth, he was a giant. The second opinion is simple, its genetic gigantism. From time to time the people with such data were born in an ordinary family. The giants united with people like themselves and built their own cities. Read the description of Goliath, whom David killed. Goliath was about 3-3.5 meters tall.

- Why haven't they survived to this day?

- Because of their wickedness, God allowed to kill them.

- It is good that today God does not apply such drastic measures to humanity.

- You're wrong. The same thing happens today. For our wickedness, God punishes us. Do you think wars, earthquakes and other disasters are just coincidences?

- I think it happened, because we destroyed the nature. We thoughtlessly wasted its resources, and this is results from our activities.

- In part, you're right. But this is not the major point. The Second World War began, because Stalin planned to destroy all the priests and Orthodoxy with them. In order to stop this madness, God allowed the war. It was not the coincidence that the war began on Sunday, when Orthodox people celebrated the Day of All Saints Who Shone in the Land of Russia. There is a story about the miracles of the Kazan Icon of the Mother of God. According to this story, at the beginning of the war, the Patriarch appealed to all Orthodox Christians around the world for prayer help. The Mother of God appeared in a pillar of fire to Metropolitan Elijah of Antioch, after he spent three days in prayer. According to Her announcement, he had been chosen to convey God's definition for the country and the people of Russia. Russia will perish if what She said is not fulfilled.

God's definition was: the opening of temples, monasteries, theological academies and seminaries throughout the country. The country's leadership must return the priests from the fronts and the prisons. They have to start serving. Leningrad cannot be surrendered. It is necessary to go through the procession around the city with the miraculous icon of the Kazan Mother of God. If they do this, the enemy will not take the city. Before the icon of the Kazan Mother of God, they need to perform a prayer service in Moscow; then She must be in Stalingrad. They also cannot surrender Stalingrad to the enemy. The icon of the Kazan Mother of God must accompany the troops to the very border of Russia. After the war, Vladyka Elijah must come to Russia and tell the truth about how the victory was won. Vladyka informed the Church and the authorities of Russia about the words of the Mother of God. Stalin promised to do everything that Metropolitan Elijah conveyed. After the procession around Leningrad, the blockade was broken, and the city was saved. There was also a religious procession in Moscow, but only here it was carried out by plane. In Stalingrad, the icon of the Kazan Mother of God stood at the forefront among the troops. Prayers and commemorations of the killed soldiers were constantly served before Her. Note, the war ended at Easter.

- I heard something about it, but thought it was a fairy-tail.
- Do you really believe that the country's atheist leadership was interested in revealing how the victory was won? The first evidence is the opening of churches, monasteries, and the resumption of church services. Second, there are eyewitnesses who took part in religious processions. One of them is a pilot who flew the plane during a flight over Moscow with icons of the Mother of God on board. In the USSR, the samizdat published the stories about these events. The author hid his name until the early 90s. I saw this story in the Orthodox Magazine "Save Our Souls". This is the journal of the Dnepropetrovsk diocese of

Ukraine. If you are interested, you can find everything yourself and read it.

■ Okay. Let's return to Atlantis. What do we have? Only Lydia's necklace remained as a proof that they have found the whereabouts of Atlantis.

■ Not only. You forgot about the artifacts that Brazilian wanderer bought up. But I don't think we can find them.

■ Why not? When we arrest him, we can interrogate him.

■ Dear Watson. We do not have a single piece of evidence that would point to this person. I hope you will not refer to telephone correspondence from an unknown American number. Plus, you've seen they covered up the black auction deals with officially signed contracts. There is not a single clue. You've forgotten about two statues which are in the American museum. Mycroft sent a letter requesting permission to examine the statue of the horse's head and the statue of Nereid riding on a dolphin for what material they are made of. Hope we'll soon receive the answer.

■ Do you think the statues disappeared from the museum?

■ No. They were replaced. It's easy to make an identical statue and replace the original one.

The ring of Holmes's phone interrupted our conversation. He picked up the phone. — Yes. ... Not even surprising. — He chuckled. — ... What do you want me to say? My guesses? I have nothing to attach to them. — Holmes hung up. — Congratulations. Lydia's necklace was gone.

■ How so? — Steve and I asked in unison. He even looked back when he could just look in the mirror.

■ Really, how so? — After thinking a few seconds, Holmes added. — Of course. Zhulikov was operating at the airport. Kravets was in Odessa. An unknown person killed the appraiser. We should have had to foresee it.

From this time, we drove in silence. Soon I fell asleep. When I woke up, Holmes was driving the car. Steve was sitting next to him. Thanks to God, we had no accident on our way home, and reached safety to Kiev. After arrival, we thanked Ruslan and his team. Holmes offered to them to have a rest before they will drove back, but they rejected an offer.

It was great to return home. It was about 5pm when we entered the house. In the living room, the served table was waiting for us. We had a splendid dinner. After a hearty meal, we stayed in the living room with a bottle of wine and chocolate.

- Where do you think Taras threw the jewels from Atlantis?
- Who knows? I am not perspicacious to give an answer on your question. We'll be lucky if someone has witnessed this event and had filmed how everything had happened. Otherwise we may never know about it. There is no other option. In five days, they could get anywhere. If we had information about their car, then we could look for them.
- Why do you so sure they used the car? They could get on the train.
- This is the safest form of transport for them. Took the train with jewelry. — He fell into the thoughts. It lasted a few seconds. Then he shook his head and continued. — I doubt that they will decide on this. In their place, I would hide in the taiga.
- Nikolayev is closer to the border with European countries than to taiga. Why did you choose for them such place for hiding?
- Elementary, Watson. They are traveling with a suitcase full of jewelry. For fulfilling their traveling, they have to sell some artifacts. In the outback of Russia, they can get hide somewhere if someone paid attention on them. But if they go to Europe, the criminal group will quickly find them there.
- Somehow I didn't think about it.

Soon Holmes, as usual, went to his lab. I went to my room for resting. I wanted to straighten up and just lie on my bed after a long drive in the car. My resting took no long time, because in about ten minutes Holmes flew like a whirlwind into my room. He looked worried. What could have happened in so short time?

- Do you want the news? Go with me.
- What are you talking about?

Holmes didn't listen to me. He left the room as quickly as he appeared. I had nothing to do, only to follow him. When I entered his lab, he was sitting at the computer. He raised his head and waved to me, inviting to look at the screen of the comp. It was the video on YouTube, which a tourist from South Korea posted on the Internet an hour ago. The video received five million views and was in the top. The tourist was on a tour of Lake Baikal when he witnessed the chase on boats. There were two people in the first boat. Two boats were chasing them. Two people were in one boat, three in the second. We were observing the full picture that we witnessed during a telephone conversation between Anton and Taras. Without doubts, the tourist recorded the last minutes of the scuba divers' life. While Taras was talking with Anton, the bandits killed Vadim and he fell out of the boat into the water.

I felt a little shiver in my body. There was a feeling that we were not in 2010, but in the distant past, when cannibals still existed. Looking at the twisted faces of the bandits, it was difficult to distinguish human features in them. They look like bloodthirsty vampires chasing their prey. When they saw that the treasures were thrown away and disappear into the depths of the lake, their faces were askew. Looking at their feverish gaze and clenched jaws seemed I could hear the grinding of their teeth. Some pursuers were swearing obscene words. Taras was almost finishing throwing the jewelry into the lake, as one bandit bared his teeth and shot at him. Taras staggered. The phone was the first to fall into the water. A suitcase and the Taras's dead body fell behind him. Everything looked like a horror movie.

■ Verily God can do any miracle. — I said. — We had no hope to find out where they went, and here it is. But what can it give to us?

■ Nothing.

■ How is this?

■ This is the end of the game, which related to the treasure from Atlantis.

■ Will not we go to find the artifacts that Brazilian wanderer gathered?

■ I am the private detective-consultant, but not the treasure hunter.

The ring of Holmes's telephone interrupted our conversation. It was Mycroft. Holmes switched on the speakerphone and asked without delay:

■ Any progress in the investigation?

■ No. Except your result, we found nothing new. We spotted Zhulikov on the cameras at the Nikolayev airport when he was boarding a plane, flying to Turkey. It was hard to recognize him, because he put on a wig and glued the mustache and beard. After using the special program, it found a man who was on 80 percent similar to our suspect. The circle is complete. From Turkey, he could fly anywhere with fake documents. Hardly we would find him.

■ That's true. Did you find out how the co-pilot got the connections with the professor?

■ According to his wife, he is addicted to gambling. Recently, he played in a closed secret club. During the game, they faked the results. The co-pilot lost a hundred thousand dollars. They threatened him if he rejects to work with them they will kill his family. His wife does not know who these people are.

■ Again a vicious circle.

■ It looks like it. We faced the same problem during the investigation with the death of appraiser. The police found nothing.

■ What about Murzyan?

- The prison officer accidentally deleted the camera recordings when he was transferring it to archive files. As punishment, the chief of the prison deprived him of the bonus for six months.
- The negligence of a prison officer alarms me, and such stranger punishment. Hmm. Interesting. So, we can consider disappearing the recording as the confirmation it value. Obviously the recording scared someone to the death. Perhaps Murzyan's death had happened not during the stroll hours. They tortured him, and he died of a drug overdose, or simply could not stand the torture. — Holmes told Mycroft our conversation with Tyutkin.
- Most likely. They could easily fake his death by stabbing after his actual death. Unlikely pathologists pay a lot of attention when performing an autopsy on a prisoner. I am sure we'll never cover the secret of this story.
- Maybe, maybe.
- And one more thing, Sherlock. I fulfilled your demand about Murzyan's case when he was sentenced to 10 years' presentment. They attached no documents to the court decision. There is no evidence, which confirmed his guilt of hiding secrets of state significance. Moreover, the judge who signed the decision was then on vacation abroad. It means someone fabricated the court decision.
- That is, the court decision is just one sheet of paper?
- Well, not exactly one sheet. They stretched the written nonsense into ten sheets. According to their piece of "art", the court could put Murzyan to prison for a maximum of half a year, not more.
- Impressive. I found the video of how the scuba divers died and sent to you. It will help you find the men, which were chasing them. The detective from Odessa called and announced about disappearing the Lydia's necklace.
- Really? That's interesting. It means only one thing.
- Indeed.

The conversation between two brothers confirmed their total understanding each other from half a word. But Mycroft's news once again brought us back to heavy thoughts. I felt dissatisfaction with the fact that we were again one step behind the professor. When will the holiday be on our street?

- About what one thing were you talking? — I asked.
- The professor still has everywhere his people.
- Do you think Murzyan told them the location of Atlantis or not?
- As I told to Tyutkin, it's possible. Only time will answer on this question.
- I am curious. How Tyrin could know the location of Atlantis if he has never been there?
- You've forgotten about navigation system. Obviously Alexius made the navigation register for him. With this information, anyone can freely find the location of a sunken island.
- Where is this navigation register now?
- I hope it disappeared together with Tyrin's death, or we'll hear the news about finding Atlantis.
- I doubt Moriarty will announce this information.
- God said nothing is secret so as not to become apparent. If he finds Atlantis, this information will leak out, anyway.
- What's next? We have no clues and nothing to investigate. Is this the end?
- No. Not yet. As long as we are both alive, I mean myself and Moriarty, this is not the end.

Soon we received the news from the American museum. According to the results of the experts, the statues are made of bronze and covered with a thin layer of gold. And in sometime, Mycroft announced the news about checking Tyrin's banks accounts. According to the revision, they issued the sale of artifacts as the purchase of services or goods.

Thank you for reading my book. I hope you enjoyed reading this story. I'll appreciate if you consider leaving a review on the site where you bought the book.

About the author

Sophia is from Ukraine. She is a chief accountant with lawyers practice and over ten years' experience of working as a tax inspector-auditor. Her life was full with interesting events. From time to time she dreamed to meet the author who'll write her story. But God decided this question in the other way. One day on her way home she met her acquaintance. The woman told the story about her niece. Someone killed her. Victim's father couldn't find the truth. According to the autopsy, it was an accidental death. This story impressed Sophia. She wanted to write the documentary story. But there were not enough materials for this aim. This event had happened proximately twenty years ago. But, though, it was a painful memory for the victim's relatives. Seemed it was the end of the unfulfilled idea.

A little later Sophia found the site FutureLearn. This site offers a lot of courses. One of them is "Start Writing Fiction". It was the beginning of getting new knowledge. After learning this course, she got the Certificate from The Open University. This course influenced on her decision to write fiction. She studied many courses on this website, which could help her in author's activity. Among such courses are: "Introduction to Forensic Science"—University of Strathclyde; "Forensic Psychology: Witness Investigation"—The Open University; "Written in Bone: An Introduction to Forensic and Bio Archaeology"—Griffith University; "Fraud Investigation: Making a difference"— Coventry University; "Managing People: Understanding Individual Differences"—University of Reading; "An Introduction to Screenwriting"—UEA (University of East Anglia); "How to Make a Poem"—Manchester Metropolitan University and many others. Sophia wrote the poetry to her fourth book be herself. And she keeps learning till today.

Sophia loves reading the detective stories or thrillers. Her favorite authors are Conan Doyle and Agatha Christie. Sophia's favorite protagonist is Conan Doyle's Sherlock Holmes. In the first story she created the detective with nickname "Sherlock Holmes". The story was almost finished as Sophia changed her mind. After reading it, she felt it didn't fit to what she wanted. At this time, she remembered watching the American serial "Elementary". This story was about modern Sherlock Holmes, but with a different interpretation than Conan Doyle's. Sophia got the thoughts: why cannot I created my beloved protagonist in our day? That's how she began to work on the author's field.

The other books written by Sophia Kiev

Till the day of publication of this book, Sophia published six books in eBook and paperback formats:

"THE RESULT OF RAMPANT ANGER";

"THE BEAST SUPPRESSES THE MIND";

"THE BRUTALITY HAS NO LIMITS";

"THE CRAZY BUSINESSES OF THE EVIL";

"THE MONSTER IS IN AN ACTION";

"EVIL HEART CRAVES APOCALYPSE".

They are all available on the site Amazon.com.

Printed in Great Britain
by Amazon

75588951R00098